
ONLY BLUFFING

JUNO CHASE

ISBN: 978-1-947234-08-6

Print ISBN: 978-1-947234-23-9

Love is the only force capable of transforming an enemy into a friend.

Martin Luther King, Jr.

Chapter 1

*E*leanor did not like games. She did not like sweat. She did not like being disheveled. Games were for children and the small-minded. In the office bathroom, Eleanor changed into a pair of black athletic shorts and a white T-shirt. She was petite and thin—in shape but not the sporty type. She was due at the softball park by 6 p.m. to participate in a city-league intramural softball game. She had agreed to run in meaningless circles to chase a ball the size of a grapefruit. And get sweaty. All because of another game.

She hired an Uber using an app. When she got in the car, she used her smartphone to look up a website describing the basics of the game. It had been awhile since she had played, and she wanted to refresh her knowledge. She brushed at the back of her neck, ruffling her short, white-blond hair with her hand. The rules were straightforward and easy to follow.

The Uber driver dropped her off. She walked the short distance to West Potomac Park, Softball Field 7. The weather was great--a smidgen of clouds in a perfect blue sky--but she was twenty minutes early. The park was nestled on a strip of land between the Potomac River and the Tidal Basin. Directly across from the Tidal Basin was the Washington Monument. To her right was the Jefferson Memorial, and to the left was the Lincoln Memorial and Reflecting Pool.

This isn't logical. I shouldn't be here. And yet here she was at a random softball park on a Tuesday evening. *Why had she agreed to this?*

She knew the answer to that. Monument BINGO. *Another* game she'd accepted. Eleanor let out a slow breath and surveyed the sparse grass.

Madeline Asher, the PR manager in the congressional office where Eleanor worked, had created a game called Monument BINGO to decide who would attend the SUNFLOWER meeting in Las Vegas. The meeting was a secret collaboration between the congressman and renewable energy innovators and would be a major career move. Congressman Pierce wanted his team to choose an individual to accompany him. Instead of picking the most qualified person-- *which would be the logical thing to do*--her officemates had decided the winner of Monument BINGO would work the Vegas meeting.

In order to win BINGO, Eleanor would have to kiss five different men at five different Washington monuments. Someone--she couldn't remember who-- had mentioned the dangers of the game, such as getting caught by the media. Then Lizbeth Crandall, the congressman's committee liaison, had implied that Eleanor might get caught. That's when Eleanor decided to play to prove her colleague wrong. She was caught up in the emotion. *Where was my logic then?* Nothing good ever came from a rash decision based on emotion.

She softened her own harsh words with the real reason she was willing to play: to meet Jack Donohoe. He was an industry leader in the automotive world. When she was young--eight or so--Tutti, her dad, taught her everything about cars: how to change the oil, check spark plugs and other basics. Eleanor used to see the Donohoe name on car parts, and the name meant quality.

But after Tutti died, even the smell of motor oil evoked too many memories, and she avoided anything to do with cars. Besides, she didn't have time to do her own oil changes or tinker around. In college, she earned a degree in computer science because it was easy for her, and she was good at it. Her mother wasn't thrilled with the choice. She preferred something traditional like a lawyer or a doctor. After Eleanor graduated, odd luck had presented the opportunity to run the Information Technology (IT) department for Congressman Pierce.

Lately, she'd been thinking about her dad. A lot. Just a few nights ago, she had a vivid dream about him. The idea of getting involved again in cars seemed crazy; she couldn't give up a job with great health insurance to pursue a dream she'd had as a kid. But life had a funny way of answering questions. The BINGO game presented an opportunity.

If she won BINGO, she'd have an opportunity to meet the Donohoe family. With that contact, she could get a job with his company. Not just any job—she could look that up on the company website and apply. No, she was talking about a job her mom would be impressed by. A job with the Donohoe family would be a smart move and show her mom that she had honored her time with Tutti. Maybe playing the game wasn't appropriate, but her mom didn't need to know about BINGO.

First, she had to win. She approached the game with the efficiency of an engineer and had already scored a kiss from an ex-boyfriend. A boring, mechanical kiss. There was nothing in the rules that said the kiss had to be interesting or fun. Besides, she wasn't playing for the ability to randomly kiss men. She was playing BINGO because Liz had challenged her. And because she wanted to meet the Donohoe family.

She didn't like the idea of having to kiss five guys, but kissing was boring anyway. She had hope that someday she'd find someone who could turn her on, but it hadn't happened yet. Her ex was a nice guy, but sex was awkward and perfunctory. They broke up soon after. The experience turned her off from wanting to pursue anything more. A kiss was only good for one stamp on her card. Anyway, it wasn't for fun and certainly wasn't how she wanted to meet men.

The next kiss was proving difficult to get. She was a natural homebody and didn't know many people in town. Her focus on IT didn't give her the broader connections of others at her office. So, when Cheyenne LaFleur, another staffer at the office, invited her to play softball with a guarantee she'd find a BINGO kiss---from a plethora of good looking, hot men--- Eleanor had readily accepted. Even though she hated games.

Eleanor watched as a couple guys placed three square cushions of white at the corner bases and a plastic pentagon for home plate. Well-worn dirt paths outlined a diamond shape, the path she'd have to run around. One of them tossed a towel on the ground for a pitcher's mound. She knew how the game was played.

Baseball and softball were a staple of any Midwest childhood. She didn't know that when she had moved from a small town in the mountains of Poland to the flat, corn fields of the US. But she learned quickly. Hopefully, this meaningless game would prove beneficial. A means to an end.

"I'm glad you came," Cheyenne said, coming up from behind her. "I didn't think you would actually make it."

"I am here," Eleanor said matter-of-factly. She held up a six-pack. "I brought beer. It's from the Okocim Brewery in Poland."

"I've never had Polish beer before. I brought Miller Lite. Everyone shares. Let's go pop it in the cooler. C'mon." As they walked toward a red Coleman cooler, Cheyenne nodded toward two men in their late twenties standing nearby. "Those guys are on our team, and they work for Congressman Manning. They are totally hilarious. Wait 'til you meet them."

"Is that the guy you mentioned?"

"No. His name is Daniel. He is playing for the other team. We're part of the staffer team. We're playing a team of Latin American foreign dignitaries and embassy workers. It should be fun. And--"

"And hopefully I will get a second stamp on my BINGO card."

"Shhh." Cheyenne stopped to lean in close and

dropped her voice to a whisper. "Geez, Eleanor, you can't talk about that so openly. No one can find out about BINGO."

"I *know*. I helped Madeline destroy the files." Eleanor stretched out her hand and regarded her unmanicured but well-kept nails. She was annoyed at Cheyenne's response but didn't want to show it.

"Let's get a drink," Cheyenne said, heading to the cooler. She popped open one of her Miller Lites and talked comfortably with the men. Flirted with was probably a better description. Eleanor wished she could be so comfortable with other people. It was easy to see why Cheyenne played. Her taking part in the BINGO game was understandable. She was friendly and a natural flirt. But the rest of the congressional team's reasons were harder to surmise. Even her boss, the rule-follower Katherine O'Malley, had agreed to play. Eleanor shrugged. Human logic wasn't straightforward like code.

"Eleanor, let me open that for you," Cheyenne said as she removed the cap with a bottle opener. Most of the players had showed up to play and were standing nearby. It was an even mix of men and women, between mid-twenties and early thirties. She heard a smattering of Spanish and what she assumed was Portuguese because it sounded different, even though she couldn't tell the words apart.

"There's Daniel now." Cheyenne pointed toward a handsome man in the parking lot who was headed their way. "He's the embassy guy, the one I told you about."

He was Eleanor's opposite. She had the lean muscles of a ballet dancer, while he had the stocky muscles of a soccer player. His skin was olive brown; hers was the color of fresh cream. His hair was jet black. Her hair was blond, almost white, the color of snow.

"He looks a lot older than me."

"He's in his mid-thirties. Not that old, Eleanor."

He waved from a few feet away. A necklace with a small pendant of a Catholic saint dangled barely visible under his polo shirt. Eleanor recognized the oval shape but wasn't close enough to identify the saint, not that she necessarily knew them on sight.

"Is he Catholic?" she asked.

Cheyenne looked around her. "What is wrong with you, Eleanor? You can't say stuff like that."

"They can't hear me," she said, glancing to the players who had congregated in a circle away from them. "Is he Catholic?"

Cheyenne let out a resigned sigh. "I don't know. I don't pay attention to that sort of thing."

"You know I'm Jewish, right? My mother would

have a heart attack if I dated someone Catholic." She said, toying with the pendant of her necklace.

"Lighten up. You're not going to marry him. Just a wee kiss on the lips at the Lincoln Memorial." Cheyenne took another drink of her beer. "Does that stuff really matter?"

"I'm not sure if I should kiss anyone who isn't Jewish."

"That sounds awful. I mean--I don't get it."

"It would feel as if my mother were looking over my shoulder," Eleanor said, holding herself perfectly still to not elicit any emotion.

"How old are you? You still listen to your mom's dating advice?" Cheyenne asked, the tone sounded as if she were partly teasing, partly in shock and partly serious.

Eleanor didn't reply. She looked down at her soccer shoes, feeling out of place. Cheyenne wouldn't understand. Cheyenne's mother hadn't told her since she was a teenager that her goal in life was to find a good Jewish boy and get married. Cheyenne didn't have to adhere to her mother's wishes, because they seemed to respect on another. Actually, Cheyenne and her whole family were tight-knit in a way that made Eleanor jealous. Most Friday nights, Cheyenne begged out of happy hour because she had a family dinner to attend. She was always talking about her mom in upbeat and chipper terms. She eagerly took her mother's phone calls. Eleanor felt a pang of longing to do the same; she wished she could be close to her mom.

After Tutti died, her mother had moved them to the U.S. when Eleanor was twelve and her mother was already in her mid-forties. It was hard enough being Polish in a new country, but also her mother was much older than the other moms. Kids teased her about it, saying she had "grandma-the-goat" for a mom. But back then, they only had each other and not a lot of family left in Poland. If Eleanor had a dime for every time her mother reminded her they could never count on anyone else, she'd be rich. To make her mom happy, Eleanor did everything she asked. Everything, that is, except find a nice Jewish boy to settle down with. But Catholic? Never a *goy*--never a non-Jew. Catholics were out of the question, at least according to her mother. Don't even bother kissing them.

"Okay," Cheyenne said, sighing. "You know ... being a rebel is *always* a good reason to kiss someone."

Daniel finished talking to his friends and looked toward Eleanor and Cheyenne. He jogged across the lawn. "Cheyenne, good to see you again," he said, his words heavy with an accent. He gave Cheyenne a quick buss on the cheek.

"Daniel, I want to introduce you to my friend and co-worker. This is Eleanor Winslow."

The corners of his full lips turned up into a smile, and his eyes wrinkled. A real smile. "The pleasure is all mine." He grasped Eleanor's shoulders and kissed each cheek European-style. She responded as she should, air kissing his checks as he did hers, but she felt giddy. The slight brusqueness matched with the tender kiss was exhilarating. His skin was clean-shaven. She imagined honey falling from a spoon into a cup of tea. He smelled sweet but with a dose of muskiness that reminded her of the pines and mountains back home in Poland.

Eleanor raised her eyebrows. She usually didn't get worked up over men, but something about this guy made her pause. His greeting, the gentle and chaste peck of a stranger, was more enticing and exciting than any embrace she'd had lately, which had been clinical, technical, perfunctory. This physical reaction was a rare response. If his cheek kisses could excite her, what would a real one be like?

"Did I do something? Can I help you?" he asked.

"What? No, I don't need help." Why would he ask such a strange question? His teeth were white, but not blue-white fake, and straight, something else that inexplicably attracted her. The directness of his gaze made her face hot. She hoped it didn't look like she was concealing something.

"Daniel Prado is from Argentina," Cheyenne said.

"He's from a small town out there, a *vaquero* from the *campo,* I believe."

"My grandparents had a cattle ranch near Baradero, by Buenos Aires," he clarified.

"*Vaquero* equals cowboy?" Eleanor asked.

"*Una mujer que habla muchos idiomas tiene un agarre fácil en mi corazón.*"

Eleanor raised one shoulder, unsure how to answer. She knew *corazón* meant heart, but she didn't speak Spanish. Was he trying to tell her something special?

Cheyenne pulled at Eleanor's arm. "C'mon, we're gathering into our pre-game huddle. See ya, Daniel."

"It's been a pleasure, ladies."

"Off you go, Danny boy," Cheyenne replied, swatting him on the arm. "Eleanor, Daniel is our mortal enemy now. We must crush him and win this game." Cheyenne raised her fists to him in mock anger.

He walked to home plate. Eleanor watched him go, unable to take her eyes away from his body: the muscular legs and a nicely shaped rear.

A coin toss settled the decision of which team would bat first. "Okay, everyone!" yelled a tall blond man who stood by the pitcher's towel. "We're getting started! The Distant Lands Dignitaries team"—he pointed to the team wearing dark blue shirts who had started to whoop and applaud—"will be playing the

Midwestern Important People in white--MIPs for those of you who are new."

Around her, Eleanor's teammates in white T-shirts started to chant, "R*ah, rah, rah!*"

"Jenny over there is taking score. After the game, we'll head to a nearby bar. Losers buy for the winners. Let the game begin!"

After a practice swing, Daniel winked toward Eleanor. "I am definitely the enemy."

Eleanor felt herself blush. Was he flirting with her? She wasn't sure what to say.

"Eleanor, come on," said Cheyenne, "team strategy meeting."

The MIPs gathered into a loose circle on their side of the softball field. Cheyenne made introductions. Everyone knew each other, so it was awkward being the new person. But they were all welcoming with friendly handshakes.

"Eleanor, what position do you want?" asked Cheyenne.

She cleared her throat. It had been a long time since she had played. Staying away from the main action of the game would be safest. "Out of the way would be best."

Cheyenne tossed her a mitt. "Outfielder behind third base."

As they warmed up, Eleanor realized the game

wasn't as awful as she remembered. The oversized glove made catching the ball easier and padded her hands. Her teammates chatted as they tossed the ball back and forth across their circle. It wasn't much to go on, but she'd get through the game without embarrassing herself.

The crowd clapped and cat-called each other. The Dignitaries were up first. Eleanor tentatively walked to the outfield behind third base. Daniel Prado was up first. He swaggered up to the plate, but Eleanor could tell he wasn't serious, that it was a funny take on male braggadocio. His stance suggested he didn't play softball much either, but his bravado was charming. He held up the bat, ready to swing.

She dropped into a ready-position, mimicking the other players on her team. She hoped he would swing and miss. Or, if he did hit the ball, that it would go the opposite direction away from her. The pitcher lobbed the ball, and Daniel swung. It went up in the air and headed straight for her. She moved back, trying to gauge the trajectory, holding the mitt above her face. All her senses were aware now. With a soft thud, the softball bounced off her mitt and rolled in front of her. She bent, scooped it up and made a split-second decision to throw it to the pitcher instead of the first baseman. Daniel crossed the base, and the referee called him safe.

She should have thrown the ball to first. Her teammate there shook his head with amusement as he clapped Daniel on the shoulder in a friendly way. Daniel caught her staring and tipped his hat. She replied with a huff, but a grin tugged at her lips. He returned the smile, but it turned into a laugh. She chuckled with him. She was impressed with Daniel. Usually men didn't do well with her countenance. She wasn't a high school cheerleader, all cotton candy and happiness. She was direct and often times reserved, a combination that often got her called names behind her back. Cheyenne lovingly called it RBF: resting bitch face. But Daniel brought out her lighter side, a side she hadn't felt much since moving from Poland.

The next batter scored a one-base hit. Daniel was on second now. He turned and made eye contact with her, then winked. *Oy vey!* She couldn't help it. The pitcher threw the ball, but the throw was high and outside. Daniel leaned forward, getting ready to run. His thigh muscles were thick and well-defined. Even the hairiness of his legs was exotic and sexy.

The crack of the softball surprised Eleanor out of her thoughts. There it was, moving fast toward her. *What the hell?* She specifically had asked to be in the outfield so she wouldn't have to play much, and here came the ball *again*. She put her mitt out to catch it, adjusting for the last fumble. This time it landed with a satisfying thump. She closed the mitt. She had caught the ball! But no time to celebrate, Daniel had already passed third. She threw it to the redheaded catcher. Daniel slid the last couple yards. Dust flew from both sides. The catcher caught her throw and tried to tag him out, but it was too late. Daniel Prado had scored the first run.

His teammates swarmed him, someone helped him up, and he high-fived all the exuberant members. As Eleanor watched, he still managed amidst the congratulatory well-wishers to make eye contact with her. Once he did, he gave her a slight bow. She couldn't help but like him, not that she would give him any clue. He already had her attention but no use letting him know. She wasn't a girly flirt.

The game went on. And on. By the fifth inning, Eleanor was really appreciating that soccer had a 90-minute time limit. In softball there seemed to be no end. The breaks and time-outs in this game mystified her. The fact that people could argue about a ball's path up or down a few inches drove her nuts. And yet this game was highly social in a way soccer was not; at least she could understand why people liked softball. This particular game was fun. The camaraderie made it enjoyable. The icing on the cake? Daniel paid attention to her. Almost every time she checked, he was staring back at her.

While her team was at bat, she grabbed one of her beers from an open cooler. He was Catholic. Kissing him should be off limits. But Cheyenne was right. Why was she adhering to the old-school rules her mother had set in place? She had been told for so long that dating, and the physical aspects of dating, were a precursor to marriage. Even a kiss was important. But she wasn't going to marry Daniel. They barely knew each other. It was presumptuous. She could kiss him. Get the next stamp on her BINGO card and move on.

By the end of the sixth inning, the two teams were evenly matched. Eleanor walked up to bat for the third time. The first two times she had missed the ball entirely. Striking out had been disappointing because she had to go back to the bench instead of running around the field like everyone else. She didn't mind losing the lap around the field. But she wanted the chance to run to second base---and by Daniel.

Cheyenne handed Eleanor a different bat than the one she'd used before. "You need to relax. You're swinging super tight. Even if you strike out again, it's no big deal. It's all about the fun, okay?"

Eleanor did not like being patronized, but she knew Cheyenne was trying to help. She took the offered bat and swung it a few times. It was lighter, the grip more comfortable. "Thanks." She strode to home plate, aware her entire team was counting her as their first out of the inning. She rolled her shoulders, trying to loosen up.

"Choke up on the bat," Cheyenne yelled, gesturing to her.

Eleanor adjusted her hands and bent her knees. She was ready this time. She was going to hit the ball.

The pitcher sent her an easy one. Maybe he felt sorry for her or assumed she'd miss again. She swung. The ball connected, and she finished out the swing as hard as she could. Shocked, she stood and watched the ball fly straight past Daniel on second base into the outfield behind him. Cheyenne gestured wildly toward the base.

"Run, Eleanor, RUN!"

Eleanor yelped, dug her feet in and ran as fast as she could. The ball was thrown to first base right after she landed on the pad. She dusted off her shorts and genuinely smiled. Daniel gave her a thumbs up.

Cheyenne was up to bat now. The other team started a taunt: *"batter-ay, batter-ay ..."* She hit the ball. It flew up and over Daniel's head. Eleanor took off like a shot. The ball bounced on the ground. A woman fielded it and tossed it to Daniel. He spun to tag Eleanor out, but she dove for the base, missing him by a mere half-inch. The umpire called her safe.

Daniel's jaw dropped as he reached out a hand to

help her. "How did you do that?" He pulled her up with such force she almost knocked into him.

Once standing on her own two feet, she said, "I can outmaneuver you and outrun you if I have to."

His smile was deep and broad. "Oh, I see. You think you can outrun me? I'll prove you wrong."

A challenge. Eleanor put her hands on her hips. She narrowed her eyes. "Maybe I'll make it all the way home."

He stepped in closer to her, the scent of his after-shave faint but inviting. He had a smidgeon of dirt on his face, and she resisted the urge to wipe it away.

"If I catch you," his voice dropped an octave, "you have to come with me after the game."

The deepness of his voice caused her to involuntarily shiver. This cowboy would not get the best of her. *All she needed was a kiss. Not some unreliable physical reaction.* She stamped her foot on the cushioned base. Unable to resist the challenge she replied, "You won't catch me."

The next hit, the softball rocketed toward Daniel. Eleanor sprinted for third base. Daniel caught the ball between first and second. Instead of trying to tag out that runner, he aimed for Eleanor. She glanced back— he was closing fast. She ran faster and was almost to third when his mitt smacked against her *tuches*.

"You're out!" the umpire yelled.

Daniel was right behind her, catching his breath. He offered his hand for a shake. "I won."

She turned and shook his hand. "Even so, *we* are ahead in the game." What did he want when he said she'd have to come with him? Her heart raced. The idea of kissing Daniel excited her; she wanted to kiss him and keep on kissing him. *Where did that come from?* She tried to push aside the impulse, but instead she imagined his lips all over her body. Eleanor walked back to her team.

"What was that about?" Cheyenne asked quietly, glancing over at Daniel. "I think you might get your kiss."

"He said he could catch me. I said he couldn't. We bet. I lost." She shook her head in disbelief. Making bets with strange men wasn't like her at all. Neither was losing. She'd thought for sure she'd win.

"What did you bet?"

"I don't know. Probably a beer," she said, not wanting to tell Cheyenne. Not that she didn't trust her, only that she wanted to keep it private. "I guess he'll tell me later."

Daniel was surrounded by his teammates. Even though they were happy he'd gotten a runner out, they were giving him a hard time for going after Eleanor instead of the easy out on first.

"That's a shit-eating grin if I ever saw one. I guess

you're going to have to figure out how to get Daniel to a memorial," Cheyenne said, "but I don't think you'll have *any* problems doing that."

"We'll see," Eleanor said, crinkling her eyebrows, not wanting Cheyenne to easily read her. But she was intrigued. He might be fun. She had a feeling he was a prankster at heart but not immature. He was a handsome man. But no point in falling for him. She had plans to get her kiss and get out.

The rest of the game passed, and the Midwestern team won by one run. After the game, everyone exchanged high fives, including Eleanor, and a camaraderie spread with shouts of shots and free drinks. *This is why people play softball, this feeling of being part of something bigger.*

Once people began breaking into smaller groups to head to the bar, Daniel approached them. "Cheyenne, thank you for bringing Eleanor to the game. I'll see you both at Luke's Bar?"

"Even though you tagged me out, we still won," Eleanor said, giving him her best as-if look.

"Touché, Eleanor. I promise you'll be glad I tagged you," Daniel said. "When I claim my prize for the bet, the win won't matter."

He turned to leave her with her mouth wide open. What the hell kind of prize was he talking about?

Chapter 2

The two teams crowded into the bar with a festive air, including random whoops and more high fives. A hand-carved wooden sign on the wall boasted over a hundred beers on tap. A group of co-eds were ordering a round of drinks. Eleanor and Cheyenne walked in together, and the blond pitcher from their team called out. "Get over here you two! We're doing Jägermeister shots!"

"I'm going to the bathroom first," said Eleanor.

"All right. Go if you must," Cheyenne said. "Hey, there's Daniel. Now, you be nice to him but not too nice."

"Whatever," said Eleanor with a half grin before she walked off.

"I saw that smile!" Cheyenne called after her, but Eleanor didn't respond.

She returned from the bathroom and wasn't interested in doing shots with everyone. Neither, it seemed, was Daniel. She sat on a barstool next to him and ordered a Polish beer. He ordered an Argentine one. She didn't do small talk. It made her uncomfortable. Daniel didn't say a word either. He appeared entirely comfortable with their lack of chatter.

When the beer came, the bartender poured it. She took a sip of her beer and glanced up at Daniel as he took a slow drink of his beer. His lips were full, wonderfully round and red. He would be a fantastic kisser. She cleared her throat uncomfortably. Even though she was interested in the possibilities with him, all she could hear was the tone of her mother's voice and the imagined look of horror in her eyes. *Relax.* All she needed was a kiss. Getting him to the Lincoln Memorial would be easy— all she had to do was ask him to go. The real dilemma was figuring out the right time to suggest it.

Daniel licked a scant line of foam off his lips and set down his glass. "So, tell me. Where did you learn to move so fast? I've not seen anyone so *rápida.*"

"It's natural for me. I move quickly. I am also very good at poker. I only win."

"You count cards?" he asked in an admiring way.

"I would say I am precise with an excellent

memory. I'm very good at cards." She kept her face neutral.

"I can't take your word." His brown eyes teased her as if they begged her to throw care away. "I'd need proof, of course."

She pulled at the bottom of her shirt to straighten it. "I am good."

"Another challenge," he said. "Don't you worry, *galgita*, I am very good at challenges and bets."

"Hmph," she said under her breath, attempting to translate *galgita* within the context of his sentence but unable to do so. She bit the bottom of her lip and released it into a pout. "We'll see about that."

"I've tried to figure out your accent, but I can't quite place it. A hint of Eastern European, I know that much."

Normally by this time, any other guy would have reacted to her acerbic conversational style by gulping down his drink and locating the nearest exits. She knew her personality was strong, but she wanted someone to accept her for who she was. With Daniel, she felt that she could be herself. She held up the beer to show him the label, which had a faded picture of the mountains on it. "I grew up in Poland--Southern Poland--in the Carpathian Mountains. When I was twelve, we moved to America, a flat country with corn and cows."

"Not all of America is flat, you know, but it must have felt that way. Was it hard to leave?"

"Yes." She looked away, unwilling to relive the memories. "And no. I was young. I got used to it, I suppose. I miss skiing."

"You ski?" he asked, drawing her back.

She turned to face him. "I haven't skied in a long time. These are hills. I am not skiing here."

"You've never been to Colorado? Or Jackson Hole? Big Sky?"

"No, I am busy with work. And it's too far."

"You should go. It's worth it. Not even Vermont?"

"Who will I go with? I don't know anyone here who can ski."

"Sure, you do. You know me."

She wanted to kiss him at that moment but instead wrapped her hands around her drink and glanced furtively at his necklace, a Catholic pendant. He could only ever be a kiss. Only a kiss. Win the game. *Ask him to go now. Before you lose your resolve.* Get in a cab and go to the memorial.

But I want more.

She shook her head and changed the subject. "Um, where did you learn to play softball?"

"I believe you must play the game–baseball, yes?-- to become American. His expression was slightly sardonic. "They are similar. I prefer soccer, but I go where the fun is."

She liked the way he teased her, always making light, but he did it in a way that made her comfortable, unlike the cynicism that underlined the sarcasm she had grown used to in her life, in this town, from her mother, in her own mind. His tone held a sense of invitation rather than an edge of judgment.

Eleanor met his gaze and lifted her chin. "Why did you come for me instead of tagging the man at the other base, Mr. Prado?" In the light, she could see flecks of warm gold and moss green in his eyes. *So this is what they call hazel eyes.*

"I don't like easy prizes."

The intensity of his gaze warmed her skin.

"Then you have met your match. Because I do not like easy prizes, either." They were sitting next to each other, slightly apart but facing. There seemed to be a pull from him, something that was warm and safe but electrifying too. Eleanor ran her fingers down her throat to her necklace. His eyes followed her hand. He swallowed hard. His dark eyes met hers. She wanted him despite her concerns. And not just a kiss but all of him. Clothes off. Bodies ... Her lips parted. He started to lean in.

"Would you two stop? Jeez, get a room!" Cheyenne interrupted with a smile. She draped her arms over Eleanor and Daniel. "I knew you would hit it off. Like ice and fire," she said, squeezing the two of them.

Eleanor did not like to be so easily read and politely smiled at Cheyenne.

"Aw, come on, Eleanor, that was funny."

"Hmph, you are a comedian," she replied, deadpan.

"I love when you let me know I've said the right thing."

Eleanor smiled at that one. She did like Cheyenne. She was a lot like Daniel, someone who understood her and accepted her for who she was.

"Excuse me, ladies. I'm in need of the men's bathroom. I'll be back." Daniel nodded to Eleanor. As he stood, his hand brushed the top of her thigh, making her catch her breath.

Cheyenne waited until he was gone. "Sooo. Are you going to kiss him? It sure looks like it."

"I might."

"Are you going home with him tonight?"

"What is this preoccupation with sex? It's sex." While she was attracted to Daniel, it wasn't going to change her beliefs about the nature and purpose of intercourse. Her mother had explained it to her in such clinical terms that Eleanor had assumed it was like blinking your eyes or brushing your hair. And Eleanor was right. Her first time was exactly like that. A nagging doubt made her think Daniel would be different. She bit her lip to dismiss the notion, to dismiss Daniel.

"What are you saying? Sex is boring?" Cheyenne asked.

"Sex is nothing. When you are with someone, it is like a business arrangement, like marriage is."

Cheyenne looked at her sideways. "Um, no, it's not. Trust me. Do you really think you'll just kiss Daniel? I think you might do more. I know I'd do more with him."

"Don't be ridiculous. It's just a kiss. There is no more than that." It was time to stop debating about whether or not it was right. She wanted a kiss. She wanted to win BINGO. Period. The end. She eyed the exit and wondered how long it would take to catch a taxi, drive to the Lincoln Memorial, kiss, and then say goodbye. Then she could stop thinking about all this nonsense. This game of kissing: it was business, not pleasure.

"Come on. He's gorgeous. Have you seen him? That thick black hair you could run your fingers through and those eyes, and he's tall, just your height. Don't forget those muscular legs you stared at through the whole game."

"Maybe," Eleanor replied, unwilling to agree even

though it was the truth. Had she really been so blatant with her ogling during the game? Ugh. It was time to turn the conversation away from Daniel. "What about that man over there, the pitcher?"

"You're looking at my next kiss. He just happens to work for the State Department, and he's always wanted to see the Washington Monument at night."

"I see. Getting closer ..."

"Yep, that will be number two."

Eleanor pursed her lips. It was still early in the game, but she wanted to win, and it drove her crazy that Cheyenne might beat her. "Daniel will put me at two as well."

A warm hand brushed along the back of Eleanor's shoulders and rested there a moment. Daniel had returned. Both women clammed up and looked at him with round eyes.

"You both look guilty," he said. "Are you talking about me?"

"Cheyenne!" yelled the blond pitcher. "Get over here! We got another round!"

"Saved by the bell," Cheyenne said. "All right, you two. Continue if you must. I'm off to give the people what they want."

Daniel shook his head as she left to join the team. "She is a character."

"How did you two meet?"

"A friend of a friend. Cheyenne knows everyone, I swear."

"She does. When did you come to the States?" Eleanor asked.

"Not until I was fourteen. My dad worked for the embassy here, so I followed him into the service."

"We are both from another country." Eleanor clasped her hands together, embarrassed. She was restating the obvious.

"We are," he said. "Sometimes America feels like a fantasy--this unreal world of democracy and Costco, and other times, I see how easily a well-established government can be snapped. After what happened in Chile, then Argentina--the military juntas."

"What happened in Argentina?" she asked. While she knew her history, she didn't know the particulars of his country.

"It was taken over by the military for a few years. It wasn't a good time for my country. It doesn't matter. My father is in a facility. Early onset Alzheimer's."

"I'm so sorry. My father has passed away."

Even though shouts of joy and companionship filled the bar, the space between Daniel and Eleanor was quiet. He seemed to understand her experience as an immigrant, unlike her American friends who sympathized but couldn't relate.

Eleanor cleared her throat. "I know similar stories

about Poland. My family did not want me to forget the past, so they, as my *bubbe* would say, 'pickled the memories in me.'"

She took a long swig of her beer. "And everything is so big--the stores, the clothes, but odd too. Almost like a different color, if that makes sense. And everyone has a way too big smile. Even so, my mother said it was safe here. Better to be safe than happy. There was a Polish pogrom in the late 60s. My mother's favorite aunt and uncle went missing. He disappeared—either to a mass grave or to the Gulag prison in Siberia. We never found out. My mom discovered her aunt's body discarded in some street like a piece of litter." Eleanor looked at her drink, swirling the glass so the foam formed a pattern along the top of the amber liquid. "I'm sorry, I didn't mean--"

"Keep going. I want to hear this. I know of the Holocaust, but please forgive my naiveté. I do not know this word pogrom."

"What?" She was irritated at first. Then she met his gaze. His eyes were wide, and she could swear they held a look of surprise mixed with sadness or regret.

She took a deep breath and continued. Most people were not racist. They simply had no idea the dark history of Jews even beyond World War II.

"A pogrom is basically the deliberate persecution of a particular ethnic group. Some of the--I guess you could say--'softer' pogroms were to simply relocate the Jews. In the late 60s and early 70s, about fourteen thousand Polish Jews were forced to leave the country." She paused to sip her drink. "My parents were included. 'Give Peace a Chance' was released by the Beatles, and my parents were forced out of their country," she said with a sardonic laugh. "They came back when it was okay in the early 90s. I was born in '94. Mom won't tell me anything. When she did talk about it, I don't remember her being sad, just very--how do you say--*it is what it is*. You do what you must. When we moved to America, we spoke only Polish or Yiddish at home. My grandmother, Bubbe, loved America, even if she wouldn't learn to speak English. They had saved her from the Nazis. But she died a while ago."

"That explains your accent. Polish and American," Daniel said, scratching the edge of his chin. "So, you are Jewish?"

"I am. My mother observes Shabbat every Friday evening and all day Saturday. She is Conservative but not Orthodox. I go with her to *shul*, but I am not as strict."

"My mother goes to church every Sunday. Catholic here," he said, making the sign of the cross on his chest. "If she lived any closer, I would have to go to mass every Sunday. You know, you and I are as different as they get." He reached for her fingers, drawing them into his smooth hand. Normally, she didn't like people touching her but with Daniel she turned her wrist so the underside was exposed. He contemplated it as if the action surprised him.

"Two sides of a chess board, black and white but somehow the same." His thumb rested on her pulse. He seemed like he wanted to say something that was on his mind but decided not to. "I want to catch you again."

The richness of his voice and the fading scent of his aftershave wafted over her, an arousing combination. He raised her wrist to his lips, and she hoped he couldn't feel the crazy leap of her pulse as he brushed against her skin. She reached for his necklace. "What is your pendant?" She lifted it to get a closer look, her fingers brushing his clavicle. "Is this your patron saint?"

Daniel straightened his shoulders and put on a serious face.

"It's Saint Margaret of Cortona, the patron saint against temptation, of the falsely accused, homeless people, and the insane," he said in a low baritone with a hint of mock sincerity. "That's my confirmation voice. I had to memorize all that when I was a kid."

"Like a bat mitzvah."

"I suppose, yes, but I've never been to one, so I can't say with certainty."

"Saint Margaret?" She let go of the necklace. "Why this saint? Did your mother think you would be insane?"

His eyebrows furrowed, but he chuckled. "I suppose you could say that. No, she gave it to me when my father got the job with the embassy. We traveled a lot. My mom wanted me to know I would never be homeless. That I would always have a home in my family." He briefly looked away. "I'm sorry, I didn't mean to go this deep. We should be celebrating your win."

She couldn't help reaching out and touched her thumb against his cheek. "I like this. Too many times the conversations are boring. This is different."

"I agree. It is nice."

"I have thought about quitting DC," he said. "Sometimes the politics are too much. But I have to stay."

"Why?"

"I have family obligations to attend to." He leaned in closer, so their foreheads almost touched, making the conversation even more private. "A curse on my family."

"What curse?" she asked. Curses were superstitious mumbo-jumbo, but curiosity drew her in. Daniel was a gothic romance in the making—a dark, scruffy Latino with a sexy accent and a cursed family. His conspiratorial tone reminded her of her favorite family friend she called Aunt who spit three times to ward off the evil eye. Every Shabbat, Aunt would draw Eleanor in close, her overwhelming gardenia perfume billowing around them, and offer up some old wives' tale advice in her raspy voice.

Daniel circled the top of his glass with his finger as if he could make music, but no sound came forth. "Someday I'll tell you, but today is not the day." He stopped fiddling with the glass. "What I would like to do is kiss you. May I do that?"

Eleanor straightened and pulled back. She wasn't used to being asked so frankly. Especially a question that evoked multiple feelings. He was Catholic. Imagining her mother's reaction sent a wave of guilt over her. But her heart pounded as if it were a ripe peach about to split. She wanted to kiss him--she wanted her BINGO kiss--but even more, she wanted to be near him. She felt so natural around him. They unexpectedly had quite a bit in common. *You always say no. Have some fun instead tonight.* She wanted his lips on hers, to have his arms wrapped around her. *Say yes.*

"Right here? In the bar?"

"Is that what you want?"

She should say *no.* But with one more look into his hazel eyes, she rebelled. She loved his confidence without bluster, so different than her own style. And the way his eyes rested on her, practically undressing her on the spot. But she didn't feel uncomfortable or dirty under his gaze. It was nice to have someone appreciate her for who she was.

"Are you claiming your prize?" she asked, surprising herself. "This kiss for tagging me out?" The audacity of her question astonished her.

"I never said what the prize was." His jaw was set, his eyes concentrating on her.

"I'm not an easy prize." She wanted to reach out, feel his strong chest against hers and run her hands through his hair, but she didn't.

He leaned into her and murmured, "No easy prizes." His nose nudged her earlobe.

Goosebumps rose on her arms, and she swallowed hard. Adrenaline raced through her blood. The feeling inside her body—a feeling that demanded release—was desire.

"Would you like to help me get a cab?" he asked, touching her forearm.

"Yes." She answered without thinking. She could go to the memorial. She could handle a kiss without getting emotional. *Who are you kidding?* The bartender brought over the check. Eleanor tried to pay for her portion, but Daniel waved her away. Cheyenne was totally into the blond pitcher, so Eleanor sent a text instead of wading through all the people to get to her.

Outside, the sun had just set, but it was still light out. "It's really hard to get a cab here. I don't know why. Let's walk a few blocks down," Daniel said. He held her hand as they walked, and she wrapped her arm around his. It was so nice to not have to think, to just have him here with her.

He put his arm around her waist and pulled her close to him. She was safe with him, she wanted him and none of the other stuff mattered. She kissed him, quickly on the neck. He turned to her and she kissed him on the lips, her hand on his cheek.

Daniel detoured into an alleyway. He swung her around easily, pressing her against a brick wall. The clay was rough against her skin. He placed his forearms on the bricks on either side of her head and leaned in. His lips parted hers for a sensuous kiss. She opened her mouth. His tongue found hers. They found a rhythm, retreating and darting, a complicated dance done with no awkwardness. Her body curved into his, and he melded into her.

He lightly traced the outer edge of her ear and then down along her neck, his fingers hot against her cool skin. "I will catch you," he whispered in her ear, "but I want to wait. I want this to be special."

She swallowed hard. He caressed the side of her cheek and stepped away.

"All right," she said shakily, every inch of her body wanting his touch.

He reached for her hand, interlacing it with his. "Don't worry."

He led her to the sidewalk and held her hand as they walked to a nearby hotel.

"Don't get me wrong," he said, pointing to the hotel. "I'm not trying to insinuate anything. The cabs come here a lot. It's a good place to find one." The doorman hailed a cab for them. She opened the door and was about to get in.

"Wait," Daniel said. He pulled her in for an embrace. Cupping her face gently, he kissed her lips and ended with a gentle bite to her bottom lip. "I'll see you soon, *galgita. Chao.*"

After he released her, Eleanor wasn't sure how she found the will to stand. She got into the cab. As the car drove away, she looked back to see him standing there. Her mind told her to leave him behind, to forget him, that it was more trouble than it was worth. But her body couldn't wait to see him again.

aniel paced in the living room of his apartment in the Golden Triangle neighborhood of downtown DC. He had to ask his mama an important question. He should drive out there. It was only twenty-five miles from DC to Middleburg, Virginia. The two places were so vastly different they might as well be in different countries. DC was a cosmopolitan town and Middleburg was horse country with vast green acres. He felt things would go better if he called.

He stopped at his bookshelves and considered the titles. They were filled with South American authors; the poet Pablo Neruda sat next to the existentialist Rafael Squirru and novelists Isabel Allende and Gabriel García Márquez. First editions of *The House of Spirits* and *Love in the Time of Cholera* rested next to each other like old lovers never to be parted. These books intermingled with staunch hardcover Argentine history books and an autobiography about Pelé, the great soccer player.

The books Daniel's grandfather had given him sat in the upper right corner of his bookshelf. He wanted to pull one down, but he was almost afraid to touch them. Growing up, the summers spent on the *campo* with his grandfather were the best times of his life. Granpapi taught him how to navigate by the stars using constellations. Daniel remembered sitting by a campfire as Granpapi told stories in a mix of Spanish and English delivered in his grandfather's odd, guttural German accent. Granpapi was still alive, but his health was failing quickly.

Daniel's gaze moved across the shelf and stopped on a history book. The leather hardbound book declared that from 1976 to 1983 democratic Argentina was taken over by a military dictatorship. The history book's nebulous description--"many people disappeared"--sounded as if only a handful were affected. The vagueness hid the true significance of what had happened. The actual number of people impacted was probably close to 30,000 but could never be verified. It was unlikely that Argentine history would be re-written any time soon to accurately tell the story. Rebel parents were routinely killed by military enforcement who also took care of the leftover children, the babies. Little innocents were handed over to "appropriate" and "military approved" families without any documentation. If there was no proof, it didn't happen.

Daniel, unsure how to handle the rising emotion, picked out a poetry book. He didn't understand why American men were averse to poetry. Its precision carried a formidable strength. He opened the book to a random page. Four lines jumped out at him. A poem entitled "The Distant Footsteps" by Cesar Vallejo spoke of things passed between father and son and choices made.

> *My father is sleeping. His noble face*
> *suggests a mild heart;*
> *he is so sweet now . . .*
> *if anything bitter is in him, I must be the bitterness.*

SIX MONTHS AGO, he had received a phone call from Paloma, a member of the Asociación Madres de Plaza de Mayo, known in English as the Mothers and Grandmothers of the Plaza de Mayo. Paloma had called with an important request that shook his solid world. Unsure of how to address her favor, Daniel had looked through his books until he found this poem. He found solace then, and knew what he had to do. The coincidence of opening the book to the same words sent shivers along his neck.

The Plaza de Mayo association had a goal to help the stolen babies uncover their biological identities. Its members believed the babies, who were now adults, should know their true parents. Over the last decades, the association had found over a hundred missing children and had established the largest genetic database in Argentina to help identify individuals and place them with their rightful families. But there were people missing still.

Was he strong enough to confront the past?

When he met Eleanor, she had spoken freely about her life. After comparing her family's story to his own, he realized how much he had grown up in a bubble. His family had not been impacted when the Argentine military brutally took power in the country in 1976, aside from the fact that it was never discussed, whether in polite company or not.

"We know you are a good person," said Paloma. "Please help us. Your mother is a good person. Your father was high up in the military. His old papers or a diary might help us track the last of the missing babies. We have heard rumors from our embassy friends that your father is in a facility. If that's true, would you consider helping us?"

As soon as she asked, Daniel knew there was something he could give her. There were boxes his father had lugged around with him since Daniel could remember. They were labeled by year: 1979, 1980, 1981, 1982 and 1983. When he was little, maybe ten, he wanted to look inside the 1983 box, thinking board games were in it. He snuck in one day to look, and when he was caught, his father reacted as if he had brought a loaded gun to his office. He had exploded into a fit of anger so fierce Daniel never saw his father the same way again. The outburst made him wary. Whenever they moved, and they moved a lot during Papi's embassy career, Daniel always looked for the box. He always made sure he knew where it was.

Why was his father so angry when he tried to open the boxes? Was Papi capable of having something to do with the stolen babies? Doubt and insecurity obscured Daniel's knowledge. Papi's job descriptions were general at best. *Your father is a colonel in the military. Your father works for the embassy.* Perhaps that was why Daniel had decided to follow his father's footsteps, so he had a better sense of what Papi actually did.

Of course, he knew his father. Papi was, as Mama aptly described him, passionate. He loved his family and was affectionate with Daniel and his two sisters, always hugging and kissing. When it came to making decisions, he was clipped and efficient. The military required it. Daniel, though, had learned by watching his father. He had the ability to turn his emotions on and off, and it had served him well at the embassy. *Was he his father's son?*

Three weeks ago, Paloma had called again to request information and to urge him to take a genetic test. "You were born in the last year of the junta," she said.

"Send me the test," he said, eager to get off the phone. The kit sat unopened on a coffee table. Could he be one of the missing babies? This would be an easy way to find out, but he wanted to know the truth from his mother. *The boxes.* He had to ask Mama to give him the boxes too. Was he asking too much?

When Papi's Alzheimer's worsened, Mama had placed him in a nursing home near Middleburg and purchased a house nearby with twenty acres and a barn built in 1890. She bought a few horses to revive old memories of living on the *estancia*. Daniel came out for a housewarming and found the boxes in an unused saddle room in the barn with an old horse blanket thrown over them.

He could go there at any time and give them to

Paloma, but he couldn't do that to his mom. Would Mama, the proud and stoic Mrs. Marietta Prado, willingly hand them over? He doubted it. He was afraid of her response. He did not want to hear her cry or yell. Silence would be even worse. If she refused to speak to him--if she hung up the phone--he wouldn't know what to do.

With a long sigh, he rubbed his face with his hands, the pressure against his cheeks almost painful. He had to do the right thing. He did not want to ask Mama to betray Papi. He did not want to believe his childhood had been a lie. But it was the only way to break the curse--to let the past be free. Besides, Papi was sick now, almost beyond any memories.

It was noon. Mama should be finished with her lunch, but it was before siesta, which she still honored even though she had lived in the States for the last twenty years.

He dialed her phone number and let it ring. Even though she had the latest cell phone, the ringtone reminded him of the phone in his childhood home. Finally, she answered.

"I just came in from a wonderful ride, and the club had a very nice lunch."

With a deep breath, Daniel forcibly relaxed his shoulders. "There is something I want to ask you."

The silence seemed to go on. He could hear her

walking across the tile floor of the kitchen. Glass rattled.

"What kind of question?"

"I need Papi's old boxes."

"Which ones?" she asked, her voice wary.

"The ones in the barn."

There was a sharp intake of breath. "What for? What have they to do with you?"

"Mama, I got a call from the Mothers of the Plaza de Mayo," he said carefully. "They are looking for documentation. I don't know what is in those boxes, but I think it's important. The information could help families."

"What boxes?" she said defiantly. He heard the refrigerator door open, followed by a heavy sigh. A few moments later, a glass was being filled.

"The boxes in the barn. We will be okay. Papi is in the home. Granpapi is on his deathbed. They cannot do anything."

"Granpapi would find a way even from hell. And so would your father. Let the past die with him. Don't ask me again," she said and hung up.

Chapter 4

*E*leanor did not sleep well. Her body felt as if it were on fire, as if she had said goodbye to Daniel moments ago, even though it was a few hours until morning. The ache between her thighs throbbed, but quietly, like the low rhythm of a song. She'd never been this distracted, so she got out of bed early and scrubbed her kitchen floor. Even her mother would be proud of how spotless it was.

After a shower, she dressed comfortably in basic black slacks with a white button-down cotton blouse, along with a pair of olive Rocket Dog slip-on loafers. She combed her short pixie cut—no curling hair for her morning routine. Since she worked in IT, she could wear attire that was casual, but usually she limited that to her footwear. She stifled a yawn and poured a black cup of coffee. Her body was tired, her muscles a little sore, but she walked the seven blocks to her office located in the Cannon House Office Building, eager for a distraction.

The day was warm already, humidity blooming with every minute even though it was only late May. The Cannon Building was one of her favorites in town. Its continuous rows of columns were beautiful to her. Past security, she walked the crowded halls to Congressman Lincoln Pierce's office.

Lincoln's office was the first room in the suite. Chloe sat at the desk nearest him to field appointments. Carleen had her own office as well, and Kat's desk was just outside of hers. The rest of the office was open space with desk setups spaced out evenly along the windows. The older building had a courtyard in the center of the building, and so each window looked out into greenery. Eleanor's desk was near the back, which was how she liked it. People were always walking in and out of the office, so being in the back offered a bit of respite from all the activity.

Eleanor pulled out her Acer laptop and set it on her clean and immaculate desk, turning the power on. She put away her canvas messenger bag. Her computer wasn't the nicest looking one. It wasn't sleek, nor did it have any fancy colors, but it was powerful. She also had a desktop to access older systems at the office. It was connected to six monitors that could be used individually or together. The screens were not top-of-the-line. They were standard issue screens, but they made the whole setup look more sophisticated. And, last, she had a third desktop that was not linked to anything other than the power outlet. She insisted her co-workers use it to screen incoming thumb drives and other media for viruses before they were added to any work machines in the office.

Eleanor checked her schedule, and a reminder popped up for a coffee date with Madeline Asher. Everyone called her the PR Manager, but her official title was communications director. She'd heard about the seating-chart app that Eleanor had developed to help her coworker Liz manage the Chinese Gala. Now, Madeline's father, Louis Asher, who had tech connections in San Francisco, was interested. He had worked for Global Tech, a leading international IT company that built databases and software, before retiring and buying a winery in Napa. Madeline had given Eleanor several bottles of his chardonnay. Why would he be interested in a seating-chart app?

Madeline Asher arrived a few minutes later. She strode confidently to her desk, which was near one of the larger picture windows, her auburn hair swishing across her back in luxurious waves. Eleanor had always wanted long hair, but her own locks were so fine that she'd kept a pixie style since her college days.

"Shit," Madeline said, popping her laptop onto her desk. "I forgot we were going to coffee. I've got to meet with a Washington Post reporter this morning. I'd reschedule, but the journalist is heading on vacation tomorrow, and it's about Katherine's judicial hearing. Time is of the essence." She pulled her long hair up into a makeshift bun and secured it. "For God's sake, did they leave the heater on last night? Why is it so damn hot?"

"You should cut your hair short like mine."

"Let's not get crazy," Madeline said, her eyes widening in dramatic mock-horror. "How about we meet for lunch at noon?"

"Let me check my schedule." Eleanor grabbed her phone and opened the protective flap. She had purchased a phone case that doubled as a wallet, and she tucked the folded BINGO card a little deeper into one of the sleeves. She needed to get rid of it. Everyone was supposed to destroy any physical evidence of the game.

"I'm open at noon. Cafeteria?"

"Not my favorite food and no privacy, but I don't have time to go anywhere else. We'll meet there, okay?" Madeline placed a few pens and a notebook into her leather computer bag and swung it onto her shoulder. "You have to meet my dad, though, for the seating-chart app. We'll talk specifics at lunch."

A week ago, Eleanor had created a program for Liz, a committee staff member in charge of foreign relations for Lincoln's office. She needed a seating chart to help her organize the Chinese Gala meant to introduce Chinese leaders to important business members of Lincoln's home state. Eleanor created a seating-chart app that was a variant on the ménage problem, a mathematical calculation on how to seat couples at a dining table so that no one sat next to his or her partner. More important, she added specific functionality per Liz's request—like the ability to *not* seat Senator A next to his ex-mistress or Senator B. Managing complicated diplomatic relations was much like handling an extended family with all its weird quirks.

Madeline had suggested the app would work perfectly for wedding organizers. Eleanor hadn't thought of selling her work, but Madeline mentioned that her dad might be interested in taking a look. He had the technical knowledge to help Eleanor place the app for sale and the marketing contacts to make it happen. Eleanor had built it on her own time and on her own computer, so there was no conflict of interest.

Eleanor's phone dinged with a text message from an unknown number. It was probably an IT issue. Whatever it was could wait for a few minutes. She stifled a yawn. "I need a coffee. Would you pick something up for me?"

"Sure, vanilla dirty chai? I won't be back until 10:30 or 11, though."

"Don't bother then. I'll get my own."

"Today is Thursday, right? No, it's Wednesday," Madeline said, answering her own question. She sat down on a chair across from Eleanor's desk and lowered her voice. "I had a kiss this morning and am setting up some dates already. Don't be sad if I win by the end of the week."

"Ha, ha." If Eleanor didn't get moving, Madeline was going to win. She needed to step up her game.

Wanting to change the subject, she asked, "You around this weekend? I'm free. We could meet your dad."

"I'm not sure. Let's talk this afternoon. My sister wants me to visit her in New York for the weekend. She has a new baby. My niece is the cutest, sweetest thing on the planet, and I can't get enough of her." Madeline nodded toward the door. "I have to go. I'll see you at noon."

Madeline was gaga over her sister's baby? Eleanor wouldn't have guessed that in a million years. Madeline came across as a woman who worked hard and partied hard. Rinse. Repeat. Eleanor assumed her silly office games came from a lack of anything serious outside of work. Madeline seemed close to her dad but didn't talk about her mom all that much. What would it be like to have both parents as an adult? Eleanor sighed. She'd never know.

The phone buzzed again. Expecting another work request, she was not prepared for the text.

> **Daniel**: *Good Morning, galgita. I got your number from Cheyenne last night.*

Eleanor leaned back in her chair, heart pounding in her chest. It had been a long time since she was actually interested in someone. Someone who wasn't her mother's pick. Someone who was unpredictable and exciting.

Galgita. She needed to look that up. She typed the word into Google's Spanish-to-English translator on her desktop. The result yielded "glue." Image search brought up a bunch of greyhounds, but she didn't see the relevance and tried searching again on Bing. This time, the image results showed an 80s video game.

> **Eleanor**: *GM. Galgita? Why do you call me this?*
> **Daniel**: *Ah. For me to know and you to find out.*
> **Eleanor**: *Don't worry. I will.*

Daniel*: I can tell you the answer. But it will cost you.*
Eleanor*: Well? What is the price?*
Daniel*: You can only ask me in person. Are you free tonight?*

This was new. A date that wasn't pre-planned by her mother. She couldn't have a long-term relationship with him, but maybe she could still get her BINGO kiss and try to forget him. But the way he had kissed her last night was certainly not forgettable. Would she be able to stop at a kiss? She had to. The date would end at the Lincoln Memorial.

Eleanor*: I am free.*
Daniel*: Good. I will pick you up at 8 for dinner.*

Eleanor stood. She placed her phone on the desk and rubbed the back of her neck. What was she getting into?

"So, Eleanor--" Cheyenne said, seeming to appear out of nowhere. That girl was stealthy like a tomcat. She sat on the edge of Eleanor's desk. "I understand you left with Daniel last night. How did *that* go?"

"There's not much to tell," Eleanor said, flustered. "I did not get my BINGO kiss." No need to tell her she'd gotten a much more memorable one in the alley.

"Well, what did happen?"

"Nothing." Eleanor shrugged a shoulder, feigning nonchalance. She was not going to give Cheyenne anything to gossip about.

"I think I see an actual smile," Cheyenne said and smacked her hand on her knee. "I knew it. I knew you two would hit it off. Let's get a coffee, and you can tell me the details."

"I *do* want coffee." Eleanor retrieved her pocketbook from the desk. "But nothing happened, I swear."

"Mm hmm," Cheyenne said, giving her the side-eye. They started walking toward the cafe. "The way I see it, you two are polar opposites. He's dark-skinned, and you are so light. He's funny and charming, and you are, well, you're Eastern European."

"You say that like I am a sourpuss schoolteacher. Thanks."

"Not quite, but close," Cheyenne said. "You're charming in your own way. I'll bet sparks fly between you two."

"Perhaps. Your matchmaking skills are so-so."

"My matchmaking skills are pretty exceptional. You need help to get another kiss?"

"You would help me? But you might lose."

"Meh, I won't. Don't worry. It's fun to set people up. I have another guy in mind if you're interested," said Cheyenne. They arrived at the café and headed to the counter. Cheyenne ordered a mocha latte and Eleanor ordered a drip coffee, black.

"My polar opposite?" Eleanor asked, putting a top on the coffee cup. "What does that mean?"

"Most people are your polar opposite, sweetie, no offense."

"Maybe in America where everyone smiles all day long. Doesn't your face hurt?"

"Ha. Are you going to see him again?"

"He is coming over tonight to take me to the Lincoln Memorial."

"You lucky girl. Will you end up in love?"

"It's a kiss. For a game." Eleanor didn't like the stone settling in her stomach. But what *about* Daniel?

BACK AT HER DESK, Eleanor spent a few minutes browsing Reddit. Even though she was serious, she had an affinity for the funny cat pictures. It was an unlikely attribute, and one she kept private. She checked the clock. It was time to work. She pulled up several Internet search-engine screens. Her primary job was to support IT systems for the office. Her second job was to gather data and search for any info leaks.

She was known in the office for being able to dig up information on the web that no one else could find. She was a whiz using internet search criteria. It sounded arrogant—she knew that—but it was the truth. When Madeline or anyone else from the office needed data, they came to her first. Katherine O'Malley, the senior legislative assistant, had tasked her with research on three lobbyists and to be on the lookout for any postings that might influence SUNFLOWER, the super-secret meeting that was going to take place in Vegas in less than two weeks.

Lost in thought, Eleanor created a dossier on the lobbyists and began a deep-dive research for the press reports. Her calendar reminder dinged. It was fifteen minutes to noon and her lunch with Madeline. She loved following information trails and seeing where they led her, bringing new data to light. The act of building a story and collating unmatched facts was like meditation. She gathered up her phone and locked her computer.

She headed down the hall toward the stairs to access the underground tunnel which connected the Cannon building to a cafeteria located in the Longworth House building. The floors were linoleum white, the walls tiled with large rectangular subway tiles, and the ceiling was a mix-mash of pipes and wiring. The tunnel was busy but not crowded. She walked quickly, her footsteps creating a light echo. Her phone buzzed.

Madeline: *Grab me a Chinese chicken salad, please, and a Diet Coke. I'm 5-10 min. late.*

Eleanor flashed her badge at the cafeteria's entrance. The place was crowded, but everyone was polite, not pushy or rude. In her opinion, the Longworth Cafe was the plainest room in DC. Her Polish public school from childhood had more color, even if it was faded. Upstairs in the congressional rooms, the design was fancy wainscoting and American Revolutionary War art, but the cafeteria was a giant space of white linoleum and cheap paneled ceilings. The walls were colorless, and even the tabletops were cream colored. True, the carpet had an actual hue--if you considered dingy gray a color. But the food was decent and convenient.

She grabbed a to-go chicken Caesar salad for herself, the Chinese chicken salad for Madeline and two cans of Diet Coke. Tables were hard to find, but a two-top opened up as she entered the dining area. She sat and opened her salad and, after putting the dressing on, started to eat. She didn't have much time, and Madeline wouldn't care.

"There you are! I'm glad I wasn't too late," Madeline said, pulling out a chair and draping a light-colored jacket over the back.

"Here's your salad. I hope you don't mind. I've already started."

"Not at all." Madeline sat, then placed her leather bag on an adjacent seat. "So, I'm excited to do this for you, Eleanor."

Eleanor returned Madeline's happy expression with a quizzical one. "Why does a winery want my app?"

"Let me start with the basics. My dad used to work for Global Tech as Chief Information Officer. He's still got great contacts. I told him about your project. He's got the winery in Napa now and does a lot of weddings and special dinners largely through and for his tech contacts. Plus, he's certain he can help you sell it."

"Should I get hold of him?"

"Yeah, he's here in town, and he's free all day tomorrow."

"I'll check my calendar and send him an email."

"Text is better. His emails tend to get left behind." The din of the cafeteria bumped up a notch as more people entered through the doors.

"Must be noon," Eleanor said. "How's everything on your end?"

"Good. Just getting my old projects wrapped up.

I'm writing up the press releases for Liz and the Chinese thing."

"She sounds busy. Is she going to play?" Eleanor looked down at her salad. A particularly reluctant piece of lettuce refused to be forked no matter how many times she speared it.

"She has this air that she's not interested, but it could be a ploy."

Eleanor regarded Madeline as if she might be crazy. Lizbeth didn't *ploy*. "I'll be at three after plans for a kiss tonight and a date later this week."

"Catching up, are you? I've got my date with Jack tonight. That makes four. Cheyenne said she has a date tonight, too. That girl is like a locomotive." She shook her head.

Eleanor glanced around the room. They were smack dab in the middle of a bunch of people who would kill for this kind of gossip on Congressman Pierce and his team. Madeline made eye contact with her and lowered her voice.

"Who is your date with tonight?"

"Daniel Prado. I met him at the softball game last night with Cheyenne."

"Nice. Is he a good Jewish boy?" Madeline asked, her voice sincere.

"Actually, he's not."

"What's your mom going to say?"

"She's not going to find out."

"Oh, that kind of date." Madeline paused from eating to give Eleanor a sly wink.

Eleanor didn't smile at her attempt to be funny but instead acted as if nothing had been said. She sipped her drink. Her phone buzzed. She had received an email with all exclamation points from Opal, one of the congressional staff assistants, whose computer had gone dead. She wasn't just some assistant though. Eleanor thought political titles were so uninspired. Opal was one of the smartest women in the office, having graduated from Harvard, and she kept the office running smoothly as a team.

"I have to go. There is a blue screen of death."

"Bye, Eleanor. Have fun on your date," Madeline said with a parting grin. "Don't do anything I wouldn't do."

Why were these girls so sex crazy? Eleanor imagined Daniel's smile, and her breath started coming faster. She dismissed the emotional reaction. There was nothing special about sex. She rolled her eyes to emphasize her internal declaration, even though she wasn't sure she believed it.

*E*leanor left work early so she could get home and change before her date with Daniel. Once inside her townhome, located north of Capital Hill, she set her purse on an industrial-looking end table. She tried not to get excited about her upcoming date with Daniel, but she couldn't help it. She glanced around the living room to see if anything needed to be picked up.

There was no clutter except for a stack of papers on her desk. She would have liked to make the place look like someone had organized it with at least an ounce of interior design, a gift all American women seemed to have. Like Cheyenne. Her place had all kinds of knick-knacks, art, and it all coordinated together to look great. Not hers.

Deep green velvet curtains hung from floor to ceiling. Square glass vases stood empty on the coffee table. She should fill them with something whimsical like feathers or glass balls. A faded loveseat that her mother had given her with a navy-blue background and white flowers sat next to a gray postmodern couch that was chosen for its sleekness and Eleanor's love for the minimal over comfort. She had tried to create some sort of design cohesion, but she liked the combination even if it wasn't Architectural Digest. It was her.

She checked her watch. Daniel would be here in twenty minutes. She felt a little giddy. *Who am I kidding?* She couldn't wait to see Daniel. She got a glass of water from the kitchen to calm her nerves and went upstairs to her bedroom. She stood in front of her open closet, sliding hanger after hanger to find the perfect outfit.

She picked out a denim skirt that showed off her long, slender legs and a red, wraparound shirt with white flowers. She laid the outfit on the bed and considered replacing it with something less sexy. But she wanted that kiss. She just wasn't sure if she only wanted a BINGO kiss or if she wanted more.

The phone rang. She checked the screen. Her mother. What impeccable timing. Eleanor certainly did not want to talk, especially tonight of all nights, but if she didn't pick up her mother would probably come over. It wasn't like Eleanor had a usual habit of being out on a Wednesday night, and she'd be worried.

"Hi, Mom." Eleanor held the phone with her shoulder as she sat on the bed. She couldn't even think about changing until she was off the phone.

"What are you doing? You sound different."

How did she do that? Eleanor hadn't planned on telling her mom about her date. She had no plans to label Daniel as anything beyond a guy she had met. "I'm going out to dinner tonight." The automatic impulse to tell her mom the truth was so ingrained that even if she didn't want to tell her, she probably would.

"With who?"

"Mom, it's none of your business," Eleanor said, her mouth opening slightly after she said it. She hadn't planned to be snippy with her mom. It just came out.

"What's gotten into you?"

"Sorry. I'm running a little late."

"Do I know him?"

Eleanor held back her exasperation. The woman had a sixth sense when it came to her. This phone call was happening exactly the way she didn't want. "He's a guy I met." Eleanor held her breath, even though she knew the question was coming.

"Is he Jewish?"

"I'm not sure."

"What do you mean you're not sure?"

"I don't--Mom, I'm running late. It's dinner."

"That's how it always starts. Even a kiss can—"

Eleanor heard a knock. "Sorry, Mom. That's him. Let's talk about it later. I have to go."

"I love you. You know I do all this for you."

And there it was. The ever-present martyr-mom reminding her, once again, that she spent her entire waking moments in service to Eleanor. Along with the words came an unspoken reminder that Eleanor should be grateful for her hard work and self-sacrifice.

"I know, Mom, I know." She tried to be grateful, but she didn't want this judgmental reaction from her mother. It was just dinner to be followed by a kiss at the Lincoln Memorial. Then she would say goodbye. Her mom would never meet him.

"Ever since your father died, I want to make sure you end up with the right person. You know this."

"I love you, too. I'll talk to you tomorrow."

She clicked the phone off and admonished herself. When Tutti had died, it was hard on her mom. And Eleanor had done everything she could to be the perfect daughter, but ... well ... when did it end? When would her mom let her make her own decisions? A doorbell chime rang through the townhouse. She glanced at the mirror. *Shit.* She still had her work clothes on.

"Hold on," she yelled, ripping off her clothes and

putting on the skirt and wraparound shirt as quickly as she could, popping on a pair of slingback heels. She glanced in the mirror and smoothed her hair and applied some lip stain. She went down the stairs and opened the door. Daniel stood there with a bottle of wine. He looked fantastic in a crisp green button-down shirt that made the green in his eyes stand out. And she knew from the softball game that beneath the perfectly fitting khaki pants were very nice muscular thighs. He bussed her cheeks with a light kiss.

Her body responded with a low buzz. She wasn't expecting an immediate reaction considering how many times she had told herself that her date wasn't anything special. "Come in," she said, welcoming him.

"Great place."

Eleanor's townhome had been built in the twenties but had random updates from the thirties, the seventies, and the nineties. Crystal doorknobs and gorgeous Craftsman design came with the home along with 1970s dark wood paneling in the living room and a '90s honey-oak cabinet kitchen.

"I bought the place when I first moved here. This one didn't have a crazy price because it was as-is with the dark wood paneling." She pointed to the feature in the living room. "I should at least paint it. But the stained glass above the doorway to the kitchen is from 1925. Someday I'll restore the place."

"Will you hire someone, or are you good at that sort of thing--remodeling?"

"I supposed I could learn how to remodel. My friend did hers by watching YouTube."

"From YouTube? That's incredible. I suppose anything is possible these days with online DIY videos." He held up the bottle. "Would you like a glass of wine? Where is the kitchen?"

"My manners . . . follow me." Eleanor led him into the kitchen. Its oak cabinets with white knobs clashed with her modern leather barstools at the breakfast bar. She would love to rip it all out and put in cement countertops. One day. At least the counters were wiped down, and the kitchen floor was extra clean from her late-night distraction--who now stood in the kitchen.

Alone. With her.

Get these thoughts under control, Eleanor.

She pulled out two unmatched wine glasses. One she had inherited from her grandmother. It was the only survivor from a set her grandmother had brought from Poland. The other was from a winery in Virginia where Eleanor had attended a festival.

Daniel opened the bottle and poured the red wine.

"I made reservations online, but I'm not sure if they went through. I can—"

"I have my phone right here. I can call," Eleanor

said as she opened the case to her phone. The BINGO card flew out and landed on Daniel's foot. She reached for it, but he was faster.

"What is this?" he asked, bringing it in closer to read.

"Oh, that. It's nothing." She tried to spirit it away, but he moved it just out of her reach.

"Let me see. FDR Memorial and a lobbyist?" He scratched his chin, his eyebrows furrowed, but a smile played at his lips.

"It's nothing. Give that back," she said, reaching for it. He lifted it away again.

"Armed Services member at the Washington Monument? I've never seen a game like this."

"Daniel. You give me that right now." Eleanor wasn't playing games with him anymore. Her eyes narrowed, and she used the most authoritative voice she could muster. "I. Am. Serious."

He raised an eyebrow as if he had caught her being naughty. "A BINGO card game. I see it has your name on it. Monuments, job titles?"

Eleanor's initial response was to lunge over the countertop, snatch it out of his hands and tell him to mind his own business, but she decided to play it cool instead. Nothing drew more attention than over-reacting.

"It's just a game I am playing," she said, with a

slow sip of her drink. She picked up her phone to distract him. "You should see this." She held out the screen. "These cat pictures are so funny."

"That is the worst diversion I've ever seen." He tapped the card and looked at her with mocking enthusiasm. "And here is my position listed, a foreign dignitary or embassy. There's a location, too, the Lincoln Memorial." He paused to look at her, his gaze intent. "Tell me more about this little game."

"Oh, well, you know. Nothing." She tried to take the card from his hand.

He held it to his chest. "*Mi dulce galgita*, trust me. I promise you can tell me anything."

She sat at the breakfast bar and reached for a paper plate filled with *bialys*, Jewish flat bagels with dried onions in the center, and took one. Her mother had made them from a recipe that was generations old. "I'll trade you." She held up the bread.

"Eleanor, I promise you. Trust me," he said, unrelenting.

She set the bialy down and took a drink of wine to stall for time. "This wine is good. What is it?"

"Argentine red. Better, but not quite enough. Tell me."

"It's not that big of a deal, but . . . crap. I was supposed to throw that paper out." With a resigned sigh, she said, "I'll tell you, but you have to give it to me first."

He handed over the paper. "You are not very good at subterfuge, are you?"

"No. I'll be right back." She headed into the living room where she had a desk and popped the card into the shredder.

When she returned, he said, "Now that the proof is gone, surely you can tell me."

She regarded his appealing looks, the dark hair she wanted to run her fingers through, the intense, dark chocolate-brown eyes, the hot pepper personality. She wanted to kiss him again. In the kitchen. On her couch. At the monument. In her bedroom.

"All right. I can't believe I'm going to tell you of all people."

"*Dime, galgita.*"

She assessed him. He seemed like he wouldn't judge her. "I'm playing this game with ... friends. We decided to play this BINGO game."

"How do you play?"

"You kiss a man at the monument. But it can't be anyone. He has to have the job on the BINGO card."

"I see." His eyes twinkled. "A kissing game. You have to kiss five guys at five different monuments?"

"It's supposed to be a fun thing, a way to meet people," she said, looking around the kitchen, unwilling to discuss that the game began as a work solution. "I would love to kiss you. I'm way behind. I need to kiss a lawyer, someone from an embassy, the armed services and anyone from the IRS agency."

"That shouldn't be too difficult. I am currently employed by the Embassy of Argentina, and I am obliged to help. Perhaps I could be of service finding you someone else, too. I know several lawyers." He chuckled. "My God, I can't believe I said that. Forgive me, but I truly find this game of yours quite intriguing. I want you to win."

"You want to play?" Eleanor was no good at hiding her thoughts. Her eyes were about to pop out of her head.

"Did you plan to kiss me before I knew your name? Is *this* why Cheyenne brought you to the softball game?"

"You could say it happened like that."

"You were going to take advantage of me?" he said, looking slightly amused. "How is it going so far?"

Eleanor tried not to smile, but a laugh escaped her lips. "We'll have to see."

"I think it's quite funny, actually. To be honest, I didn't think women did this kind of thing, no?"

"This is the twenty-first century. Besides, it's just a game. It's a kiss, nothing more."

"Nothing more?" he asked curious. "How many men have you kissed for the game?"

"One. He's an ex."

"How did it go?"

"It was a kiss." She shrugged, dismissing it.

"Will I be number two?"

"Yes. I also have a date on Thursday, but I'm not sure after that."

"You may kiss me. I give you permission." He loosened the knot to his tie, his eyes twinkling. She wanted to trace the tiny smile lines that radiated out from his eyes.

"Permission?" she asked.

"We are friends first. Besides, it is only a kiss. For the third kiss, can I watch?"

"You are incorrigible! No, you cannot watch."

He chuckled, almost laughing and then checked his watch. "We have to go. Our reservation is in a half hour. If we leave now, we'll just make it."

They stepped out into the balmy night and hailed a cab. Daniel did not try to hold her hand, instead resting between them on the seat. Traffic was light, and they arrived a few minutes early at Joe's Seafood, Prime Steak & Stone Crab restaurant, a relatively new seafood place in town.

The inside was East Coast neoclassical. An impressive series of arched windows lined one side of the room. Two marble pillars topped with Grecian scrolls accentuated the area, standing proud. Metal chandeliers hung from the ceiling, giving off a soft light--enough to make the place romantic, but not so little that friends couldn't dine there comfortably. From the bar, the low din of conversations and laughter filled the room.

At the table, Eleanor opened her menu and studied the list.

"Are you hungry?" Daniel asked. "Would you like to order tapas style? There are several good appetizers here."

"The appetizers look really good. I would love that. The meals look good too, but I'm not as hungry as I thought."

"Do you like oysters?"

"I do. And let's get the crab cake, the steak tartare ... Anything else?"

"Ceviche. That's should be enough. You order food like an Argentinian. A little bit of everything."

The waiter appeared, asked if they had any questions and poured water. Daniel ordered the food along with a bottle of Argentine red wine. "Red should go with steak, yes?"

The waiter took the orders and left. Daniel regaled her with tales of riding horses on the *campo*, bringing the cows in, and telling stories by the campfire with a sky full of stars against a black sky. The waiter returned with the bottle and poured a presentation glass. Daniel tasted it and nodded to the waiter.

"Malbec reminds me of home, though I have lived in the States for so long I'm not sure it is my home anymore."

Eleanor watched Daniel casually rub his pendant, the Saint Margaret. How nice to have that feeling he belonged no matter where he was. She told him of hiking in the Carpathian Mountains when she was young.

"I went up in the mountains by myself. I think I was nine or ten. No one minded," she said. "It was just different in Poland. We had more freedom to do things."

"It was like that in Argentina, too. I could be gone for hours riding my horse as long as I came home before dark."

Eleanor nodded. She had been allowed to roam fairly free until they moved to the States. Until Tutti died and her mother became overbearing. "I remember one time, it had rained earlier in the day. The valleys were emerald-green and, against the horizon, mountain peaks lined the sky. I sat on a rock by myself for hours."

"Your Carpathian Mountains sound similar to the

Andes. I've tried to hike around here, but it doesn't feel the same."

"Nothing on the East Coast really compares. The Adirondacks are beautiful, but they have no height. I went back to the Carpathians about five years ago with my mom. I don't know if you saw it, but the canvas picture above the fireplace is one I took there." She loved that picture, how the sunbeams had shone through the gray, cloudy sky.

"I did see it, but I didn't know that you took it. You really miss it," he said, cocking his head. "Then it is settled. You must come with me then. This winter, I will take you to Colorado. You must see the Rockies. They will remind you of home."

Eleanor halfheartedly smiled. She didn't want him thinking long term since it would never happen. She was a good Jewish girl and would marry a good Jewish boy. Daniel would be a kiss and then she would say goodbye. "It's funny, your name. It's more Jewish than it is Catholic."

"It is strange, is it not? Daniel who stood unharmed in the lion's den only judged by God." He took a drink of water and cocked his head in thought. "I'm not sure why Mama gave me this name. But I've never asked. The name Eleanor doesn't sound Jewish, either."

"It's not common, but it is Jewish. It means a 'shining light.'"

"I can see that. You have certainly lit something in me," he said, looking intently into her eyes.

She could feel the heat rising into her face and met his gaze for a brief moment. Then she looked away. "Um, how did you get involved at the Embassy? That's not an easy job to get."

"My father worked there for many years. It was easy to get a recommendation. And I wanted to work with him, I don't know ... to get to know him better." Daniel pushed his hair back but averted his eyes. "What about your Dad?"

Eleanor shrugged. "My dad died after we moved to the States, and in the U.S. it was different. We used to work on cars together, he taught me how to change the oil. But I never pursued any of that stuff, even though I loved it. My mom had dreams of me being a lawyer."

"I'm sorry to hear that about your Dad. I understand," he said, placing his hand over hers and rubbed the side of her finger. "Were you glad to be in America?"

"Yes and no, I guess. I didn't have any reminders of my dad around. I mean, I even missed the stupid grocery store we used to go to. But then again, everything was new." Eleanor looked down at her hand. She liked having him near her. She felt protected.

Daniel squeezed her fingers lightly. "When I was fourteen, we moved from the *campo* to the city. It was that feeling of everything being different. Smells weren't the same. The sun-warmed grass was replaced by car exhaust. Sounds, too. Sometimes, if I have slept very hard, I wake not knowing where I am and think I should be back on *el campo*. And, yes, something like sadness but not quite."

"We have had such different lives, and yet they are so much the same." Eleanor replied quietly as if the words said any louder would have too much impact.

The waiter appeared with their meals. The food smelled delicious, and Eleanor found herself surprised at how hungry she was.

"Let's eat," Daniel said, "and then we will end our evening with your BINGO kiss."

"At the Lincoln Memorial."

She watched him carefully as he took a bite. Even though he seemed happy enough to help her out with the BINGO game, shouldn't he be jealous that she would kiss another man? The question didn't matter. *He was a kiss. The end. Next topic.*

"Why do you call me *galgita*?" she asked. "Google translator said glue. I'm not sure that's right."

"Ha. *Galgita* means little greyhound. Before you judge, let me tell you why. I give you this nickname because of how fast you are. Those long legs and that speed, it is a thing of magnificence."

Long. Fast. She looked at her legs. Her body was a series of facts. They weren't often described with such adjectives, especially not words like magnificent. She rubbed her knee, her thumb caressing the dip between bone and cartilage. His tone was interesting. She didn't feel any flattery as if he thought big words would get her into bed, nor did he say it in a way that was condescending.

"I don't run, though. That's the funny thing. I hate running."

"Well, then, it won't be hard to catch you."

"Hmph, it will take a lot more than that to catch me. And besides ... aren't you here to help me?"

"Yes, I will help you. Kisses are not serious. You want only a kiss, right? Is it more?"

"No." She didn't want a conversation about expectations, not on a first date, not when there was no chance of a relationship. Relieved, she assumed they were having a friendly dinner as a precursor to a mark on her BINGO card. Her shoulders relaxed.

"Let's have a toast, shall we?" he said, lifting his glass. "To, let's see . . . ah, to winning?"

"I like that. To winning."

As they prepared to leave, Daniel pulled her chair back for her. The gesture was unexpected, but she was getting used to his chivalrous manners. He opened the door for her, too, and the air changed from air conditioned to the warm and humid air of a summer day, even though it was late spring.

When she had first moved to DC, it had taken her a while to get used to the humidity, but now it made her feel welcome, as if she had on a comfortable shawl. The sun had set, and the night was dark. Even though they were in the middle of the city, the Potomac River smelled rich and earthy with a hint of minerals and mud. She half expected to see grass and moss, but there was only concrete and asphalt.

The street was crowded. But people had a destination in mind, not a stroll. "The memorial is this way," he said, pointing. "Maybe a thirty-minute walk."

They crossed the street to the Ellipse, a park located in front of the White House. During the Christmas season, it was where the official tree was set up. They walked along a garden path, the edges lined with small lights, in silence, comfortable with the quiet between them. When they reached 17th Street, he took her hand, and they crossed.

The Lincoln Memorial glowed in the distance against the dark sky. To her, this building had always been a testament to breaking free from old ways. Respect passed through her. Even at night, the grounds were busy but not crowded. Tourists were snapping pictures and talking to each other in awed voices.

Daniel led her to the front of the memorial. They sat on the front steps of the monument, which faced the Reflecting Pool, and, in the distance, the Washington Monument. The obelisk was lit proudly against the horizon. "There's the Washington Monument. Isn't it beautiful?" he whispered, putting an arm around her.

Eleanor relaxed against him and leaned her head on his shoulder. She liked having him near.

"I love this city. Argentina will always be my home, but this place is where I grew up. Does that make sense?"

She closed her eyes. His fingers caressed the side of her jaw, stopping at the underside of her chin. He directed her face toward him. She turned her body into his, wanting him. His mouth met hers, playfully biting her lower lip.

She pulled back a fraction. "To freedom, right?"

"To freedom."

He kissed her firmly. His hands slipped under the back of her shirt and traced her spine with his fingertips. Gently, he retreated.

"You have your kiss, yes? How do you prove that you have it?"

"I have to Instagram it, hold on." She snapped a selfie with the Lincoln statue and posted it. Daniel took the phone and pulled her close and took another selfie of the two of them.

"*Galgita*, I have something fun for us to do. Trust me?"

Chapter 6

*E*leanor and Daniel arrived at the Tropicalia Lounge to the barely muted sound of drums and throngs of people coming in or going out. Small groups congregated on the street or walked on to the next place. It was crowded but not overwhelming. Once inside, they stepped up to the bar. Three hanging lights looked like giant peony blooms. They gave off a soft light, and the counter was lit up with a green she could only imagine in the jungle. The place was a nexus for people from all over the world: Latin to Caucasian and African American to Indian. Languages from all over the world bounced around her.

Daniel leaned in to talk to her over the loud music. She inhaled his scent, that light touch of aftershave and musk that reminded her of home. At once, she felt safe with him.

"Howard University is not far from here, and Adams Morgan is around the corner. I love it here." He handed her a tall glass of clear liquid with lots of mint leaves. "A mojito."

She took a sip of the sweet drink and let the flavors roll around on her tongue. "What's in it?" she asked before taking another drink.

He held up his glass. "Mint leaves and rum, a little sugar and lime. Your first one?"

"Yes," she said. "It's delicious."

"Follow me." He led her past the bar and around a corner to where the dance floor was. Next to the dance floor was a stage that held eight or nine people--men, women, white, brown, and black—all wearing a similar circular print pattern in bright white, purple, black and red.

A few people carried oversize steel pan drums hanging from their hips and were pounding out a body-shaking rhythm. Some played bongos, and a few had snare drums. Together, they produced a thrumming beat that Eleanor could not resist. She tentatively swayed her shoulders to the music, feeling it out with an awkwardness she hoped didn't show. Daniel took her hand. At first, she resisted. She wasn't good at dancing and had earned the nickname "Tinman" in high school.

Daniel pulled her toward him. "Just let me guide you, yes?"

Eleanor's body was straight as an iron rod, but she did trust him. She wanted adventure, even if her body wasn't agreeing with her. She nodded.

He led her to the middle of the crowded floor. People danced as if no one watched. Yellow and pink theater lights strobed over the floor. Sequins shook and flashed from dresses made for drawing attention. Arms were straight up in the air; hands bounced to the music and bodies curved to the beat. Daniel came in close and put his hands on her hips. His grip was solid but not tight. "The way to dance in Argentina is to first feel the rhythm."

He moved his hands so her hips swung to and fro, slowly at first, skipping every other beat. "Now bend your knees a little. Put your hands on my shoulders."

Eleanor did as he suggested and tried to move gracefully. She was stiff. She couldn't help it.

"Now close your eyes and relax."

She closed her eyes. The scent of sweat and smoky dry ice mingled with Daniel's musky smell. She let go and started to move more fluidly, swaying side to side. *Bum ba bum, bum ba bum.* It was so . . . so . . . sensual. Fear started to ride up her spine and stiffen her. Her body wasn't meant to move like this. She started to tense.

Daniel moved her hips in slow circles. "*Galgita*, you are safe with me. Relax. I know you can hear the music, but can you feel it? Let it breathe on your skin."

Eleanor opened her eyes. Daniel had been watching her hips, and now his dark brown eyes adjusted to focus on her.

"Are you ready?" he asked.

"Yes."

His hands stayed firm, but he quickened the pace, and she followed him with her body, her hips matching his moves. "That's it," he said as a slow smile spread across his face. He tilted his head to the side, a silent request to step closer. She nodded. She wanted his hands against her bare skin, his lips on her body.

Daniel's hands moved from her hips and up along her back before settling on her lower ribs. He stepped a foot between her legs. She moved closer so that her thighs touched his leg. Instead of controlling her thoughts, she leaned back and shook her head, laughing, her whole body moving to the insistent rhythm of the drums.

Daniel's hands pressed her toward his body and their hips met, swaying together as if they were already one. She had no idea her body could move like this, so naturally but in syncopation with Daniel's. His hands were like fire on her body. She smiled but pulled away enough to be a challenge still. The music emboldened her. The beat naturally helped her move until she found herself so close they could kiss.

"Your body moves well with music," he said, telling her as if it were a secret.

Only a few inches apart, tension thrummed between them. She was wet with desire for more than dancing with him.

He turned her so her back was against his stomach and she looked out over the crowd. His hands were on her hips, rocking them back and forth. *Bum ba bum, bum ba bum.* He caressed her throat with the back of his hands. She rested against him, letting his body carry the beat for them both. Her hips had taken on a life of their own, her core hot, enticing him with a primal pulse.

When the song ended, he spun her into his arms and tilted her in a gentle dip and kissed her. His mouth parted her lips and matched his moves. The whole world fell away except for the demands of the music and the luscious, sensuous lips of Daniel Prado. With a soft tug on her lower lip, he pulled away and then guided her upright.

"I've almost caught you," he whispered against her ear.

He intertwined their fingers, and they walked off

the floor. They exited the club. Cool, night air skimmed across her. He led her away from the sidewalk and pulled her into an embrace. His hands cradled the sides of her face.

Eleanor was out of breath and unable to put together two words. She was in shock, her core throbbing to the faint beat coming from inside the club. Instead of letting go, her hands went around him and pulled him closer. She didn't want him to leave.

He kissed her, his mouth parting her lips, and his hand covered her breast. He found the nipple through the fabric of her shirt, its aching flesh between his fingers. His hips dug in against hers, his cock hard. His tongue was deep in her, tasting her, wanting her.

Breathing heavily, he pulled back. "Not tonight, *galgita*. Dinner tomorrow. I promise it will be most amazing."

Eleanor tried to contain her disappointment. She leaned away, releasing the tension in her neck with a quick side-to-side movement and exhaled through pursed lips. He pushed a loose strand of hair behind her ear and straightened her shirt. She swallowed and tried to ignore her raging skin, so sensitive to his touch. He took her hand, and they walked to the closest corner, where he hailed a cab.

When the car stopped, he opened the door. She kissed him before getting in, a gentle chaste kiss on the lips, but her desire came raging back. Somehow, she got into the vehicle. Somehow, the door closed. And then she was in a cab again, saying goodbye when her body was on fire.

ELEANOR HAD NEVER BEEN in a such a daze, she still didn't quite remember the cab ride home or paying the driver or how she even made it through her front door. The sensation was wholly new, and she wasn't sure what to do. Inside her townhouse, she couldn't decide if she should drop her purse and crumple to the floor, or if she could make it to her bedroom and collapse onto her bed. Part of her knew if she chose the floor, she would be unable to get up again. The bed it was, then.

As she walked toward her room, an article of clothing came off. First her shoes. She lifted her shirt over her head and threw it on the stairs. She unzipped her skirt and let it fall. Off came her bra, which she flung onto the bannister, and then her underwear, kicked off to the side.

Her body commanded her. She lay on her bed. With her hands, she cupped her breasts, lifting and squeezing them, swirling the nipple like Daniel had done. Her head rolled back. Her hand slid across her firm belly, over her hips where Daniel had held her to her mound.

There she hesitated. She knew about masturbation, but she had never been interested. It was awkward and left her unfulfilled. The guilt of touching herself always overwhelmed her desire. Until now. The need to end the hunger between her legs overrode her misgivings. She was alone in her own bed and able to do as she wanted.

She spread herself with her fingers. Unsure of what to do, she closed her eyes and willed her hand instinctively to go where it needed. Her index finger found that part of her that needed to be touched. Her clitoris was swollen and throbbing. She circled the spot and then pressed against it, the pleasure immediate, and opened her knees to allow easier access. She passed the nub and entered her opening. She gasped and angled her hips toward the source of pleasure.

With a pinching motion, she rubbed both her clit and her opening. Her hips moved to the rhythm she and Daniel had danced to: *Bum ba bum, bum ba bum.* Her body stiffened, getting ready for an orgasm. Her legs tingled. Her eyes flew open. She stopped, scared. Her body had never responded this way. With a few breaths she caught up. This was new and powerful. It scared her at first, but she wanted to finish.

She closed her eyes and imagined herself back in

the club, back in Daniel's arms with his hardness pressed against her. She began moving her hand slowly at first, then with speed. *Bum ba bum, bum ba bum.* Her hips responded. Soon, she could feel each beat of the rising buildup. Her body tensed again, but this time she didn't stop nature from taking over. She quickened the pace. When she came, her whole body stiffened. A wave started deep in her core and reverberated through her like a stone hitting the surface of a lake. Afterwards, she slowed and came to a natural stop.

That sure as hell wasn't perfunctory. Whatever it was Daniel had planned for her tomorrow night, she was already hungry.

Chapter 7

*E*leanor slept well, perhaps the best she'd ever slept. She didn't need to take two showers or mop the kitchen floor to wear herself out to get her mind off Daniel. The day was bright and clear as she walked to work. The Cannon House Office Building was only about a half mile away. When she got in line to go through security, she didn't mind the wait. And she smiled at the security guard. An actual smile.

At her desk, she checked the daily schedule. She had meetings scheduled sporadically throughout the day, but the only event she cared about was meeting Madeline's dad, Louis Asher, for lunch. They had made plans to meet at a Mexican restaurant to go over her seating-chart app. Her phone beeped. She had a message.

Daniel: Be at your place tonight at 8.

Eleanor: What are the plans?

Daniel: First, dinner.

Eleanor: Then?

Daniel: Then we'll see. What would you like to do? More dancing?

The fast beat played in her mind--the way he'd held her, the way his hands felt on her hips.

Eleanor: Perhaps a softball game?

Daniel: Maybe you are too fast for me, galgita?

Eleanor took a deep breath. She could feel the softness of his lips against hers, insisting, wanting. Her heart was racing, but she wasn't willing to let him win that easily.

Eleanor: I am quick. But will I catch you?

Daniel: No easy prizes remember . . . I'll pick you up at 8.

Eleanor was about to schedule in her date with Daniel when she realized that she already had a date scheduled for the exact same time. A date she had made before she met Daniel with a man named Kaleb on JDate, a Jewish dating website.

Eleanor: I'm sorry. I have a date tonight. Would Friday be okay?

Daniel went radio silent. Eleanor put down the phone and started to work, but she couldn't concentrate. She was a little surprised at his lack of response. He'd known she had a date. He wanted her to win. He was even going to help set her up with others. Had he changed his mind? For the next ninety minutes, she kept clicking her phone until he finally responded.

Daniel: Of course. Friday then?

At first, she'd been glad he'd promised to help her but now? What kind of feelings did he have for her? Were they real? Was she willing to defy her mother for him if he wasn't willing to fight for her? Even so, none of that mattered. He should only be a kiss, nothing more.

CHEYENNE CAME into the office carrying a plastic-wrapped paper plate. Apparently, another early morning meeting had wrapped up. Eleanor could smell the sweet pastry goodness before Cheyenne even approached.

"I was doing some research last night, and I found this Polish recipe," Cheyenne said. "It's called papal cream cake. Have you ever heard of it?"

Eleanor shook her head. *Papal cream? What is Cheyenne getting at here?* She wasn't Catholic ... *Uh huh.* The name of the pastry was to remind her of Daniel.

"What are you trying to say?"

"Oh, I don't know," Cheyenne said, her voice

switching to a sing-song tone. "Maybe someone else inspired me." She set the plate on Eleanor's desk. "Any chance you can help me get it to the right person?"

Eleanor sighed but gave a hint of a smile. And a cream cake. As if she needed reminding how Daniel made her feel indulgent with his touch, like the taste of sweet cream.

"Do you need his phone number?" Cheyenne asked.

"I have it."

"Already? My, my, Eleanor, what will your mother say?"

"Enough of your comedian's words." She didn't want to be reminded. She didn't want anyone to know that she liked Daniel more than a kiss. Especially Cheyenne. Especially when she was supposed to move on after the kiss, and she didn't want to. She didn't want to forget him.

Cheyenne held up her hands in mock surrender. "All right, you caught me being nosey. But really? I've known Daniel for a while, and I have this feeling about you two." She crossed her arms over her heart. "You'll make sure he gets the cake?"

Eleanor narrowed her eyes and didn't answer.

"Point taken. You can thank me later."

～

AT A QUARTER TO NOON, Eleanor packed up the laptop that held the demo of her app. She walked to Oyamel Cocina, the local Mexican restaurant where she and Madeline's father had agreed to meet. As she passed by the Capitol building on her way to lunch, she knew she loved DC. The post-war buildings were built with architectural flair, and every window had an arch, unlike many of the boxy modern buildings with no style. The sidewalks were red brick, probably from colonial times.

The restaurant was located in a building with residential apartments above it. She entered the small shop, and the smell of fresh cilantro welcomed her. She was in the mood for a grilled Mahi Mahi taco with spicy salsa and an order of guacamole. *Another odd thing.* Normally she wasn't a big fan of food. Food was to feed the body fuel. A necessary annoyance. She had her favorites that her mom made, of course, but she wasn't usually that interested. So many little things were different today.

Once her eyes adjusted to the light inside the restaurant, she found Louis already seated at a booth with a margarita in front of him.

"Madeline described you perfectly," he said, standing.

"The hair, right?"

"Yep. Let's order before we get started, shall we?"

"I already know what I want," she said.

He closed his menu. "I'll trust your judgement, then." He waved the waiter down and told him he'd have whatever Eleanor ordered.

"What do you think of the app concept?" she asked as soon as the waiter was gone.

"Okay, let's get right into it. I like that. Direct. I haven't seen it yet, but from what Madeline says, it sounds useful and marketable. Tell me about it."

"It's pretty straightforward. The user enters a list of guests plus what I call 'seating requirements.' These include things like 'must be seated next to' and 'must not be seated next to' fields. Each guest can have unlimited requirements. The program then sorts through them and provides a chart that meets the parameters. It's simple, really."

"Mads mentioned you built it for one of your co-workers--Lizbeth, is it?"

"Yes. I built it to help her plan out a gala. She had to make sure all the appropriate people were seated together, and she was doing it by hand."

"As they say, necessity is the mother of invention and all that. What's the interface like? Can I see it?"

"It's loaded on my laptop. I'm working on a phone app now, but I'm not sure that will be as robust. More like a last-minute emergency application for use at an event."

Eleanor pulled out her private laptop and logged on. She opened the demo, which already contained a few hundred fake entries. "Once the guest list is added, the chart is made. It can accommodate for last-minute changes and rearrange the seating. It's really flexible." She continued with a summary of the various features, including a nifty print feature that would allow an organizer to make custom graphics for the event itself. Liz hadn't needed it, but the idea had come to Eleanor one night, and she'd added it just for fun.

"The organizer can enter food choices and allergies to create a list for the caterers and banquet managers. It's possible to seat all the vegans at one table, all kosher people at another, etc." Eleanor paused to sip her water.

The entire time she spoke, Louis had not interrupted. His questions about the program were on point and detailed. Madeline Asher was lucky to have such a kind and generous father. A tremendous longing crept up in Eleanor's throat for her own father. *Get a grip, Eleanor. This is a business lunch.*

"This is excellent," Louis said. "I think we can use it across several platforms. We can sell this to meeting planners, wedding planners, and, well, anyone who is coordinating large-scale events. May I see the source code? I want to check for scalability."

"Sure." Eleanor feigned nonchalance, but a flutter of angst swished through her. She wasn't worried that he'd try to steal it. He could probably come up with something as good or better. Her style of coding wasn't always easy to parse, but he had a CIO background. He'd either understand it, or he wouldn't. She opened the files and let him see. She wished she'd added more comments to her code for clarification, but she'd never expected to show it to anyone.

"This program is fantastic," Louis said, finally looking up. "The code is elegant. I'm liking it. Plus, it's adaptable. I did a quick Google search before I got here. None of the other apps are as accommodating, which will give us a leg up in the larger corporate markets."

"Thank you." Not many people ever saw her code. To have someone of Louis Asher's caliber compliment it like that was invigorating.

"I want you to meet up with Jay Dolan. He's one of my top programmers, and he's in DC to help me with a project. He's busy, but I'll text you his contact info. And maybe you can help me with some pro bono work I'm doing."

Eleanor wasn't used to such decisiveness. In government, no decisions were ever made this fast unless Cheyenne or Liz were debating where they wanted to eat lunch.

"What pro bono work?"

"I'm helping food banks come up with a way to share food. A food-bank marketplace, for lack of a more marketing friendly title. So, if another food bank has way too much that's about to expire, they advertise it on the marketplace. If one is low, they can request more."

"You're working to make sure food waste is minimal. Makes sense."

"Quick study. I like that. About this app," he said, tapping her computer and turning it back to her. "I'll be honest. This app will sell, but it's not going to net you millions. It will net you a solid bump. Enough to pursue a fancy hobby but not enough to quit your day job."

"Are you interested in buying my app or going into a partnership?"

"Let's discuss that after you meet with Jay. Do you mind emailing him a few samples of code?"

"Sure," she replied, sitting up. *Wow*. This was really happening.

He examined what was left of the taco on his plate. "Damn, that was good. I might have to learn how to make those. And I think this is going to work out wonderfully for us."

Chapter 8

Daniel couldn't give up on his mama. Not yet. But Marietta Prado was not answering the phone. She must be upset about the boxes he'd requested. The same way his father had been all those years ago. Daniel stood in his living room. His thumb hovered over the Uber request-ride button. He would go to Middleburg, break into the stables, and retrieve the boxes. He could take them without her blessing.

But she would never forgive him. *Who cares?* He did. He wanted to do the right thing for everyone involved. He didn't want to bully his mother. He wanted her to see reason--to see hope, to tell the family's truth.

He sighed and went back inside, shutting the door behind him. Showing up and taking things without consent was not how he did things. He dropped onto the couch, his hands on his lap, his body limp. He couldn't bear to consider the horrible things the men in his family might have done.

Granpapi had emigrated from Germany in 1948. The family name wasn't Prado, but no one had dared to ask his real last name. His official papers identified him incoming as Prado. But Daniel knew it wasn't hard to bribe someone back then. And Papi had served as a colonel in the Dirty War. Was that enough to discern guilt?

Maybe the details didn't matter. His grandfather was dying. Now in his mid-nineties, he was barely coherent in a at the family's *estancia*. Daniel's father was in his late sixties and in an Alzheimer's facility near Middleburg. The generations of willful ignorance had to stop. While he didn't want his father's name smeared, he didn't want his family name to stay dirty. Not when he knew the goodness of his grandfather or when he remembered the protective love of his father.

The genetic test from the Mother's of the Plaza Association had sent him was in his hands. He picked it up, the words re-playing in his head. "You were born on the last year of the war. We want to know if you are one of the taken children."

He twisted off the top and tipped out a plain cotton swab. All he had to do was swipe the side of his mouth, place it in the tube and mail it in. Within four to six weeks, his whole world could change. He had to know.

His family's curse was wrapped up in the history of his father and grandfather. He could still hear the raspy voice of the old woman who had delivered the curse as clearly as the day it was spoken twenty years ago. The afternoon had been warm but not hot. The sky was blue. He was fifteen years old, and his older brother Thomas and sister Camila were still inside the school, at the front door, grabbing their packs. Mama was there, ready to take them home.

They started off briskly and came to a street corner where they were supposed to wait for Papi, who would drive them back to the *estancia*. An old gypsy woman stood there, leaned over a knotted wooden cane. She had black, curly hair held back by a colorful babushka. Daniel had never seen her before, and he would never see her again. Yet she had changed their whole lives.

"Let me tell you your fortune," she said to his mother. "Your youngest boy here is very handsome. I will tell you for free."

His mother pulled Daniel away but didn't rush off. The gypsy seemed to move preternaturally. Suddenly she was next to him, smelling of incense and old sweat and lifting his hand. The unfamiliar scent had reminded Daniel of the scary fairy tales that Granpapi read—Cinderella's stepsisters chopping off their heels and toes to fit the glass slipper. Frogs hurled against the walls.

His older brother, feigning confidence, stepped between them. "Read mine."

The gypsy did not release Daniel. "I will read this one."

"Oh, for the love of God," his mother said. "Get out of the way, Thomas."

The old woman grinned. He could tell that she had been beautiful once. Her gray-brown eyes reminded him of the desert. She was missing teeth, and the ones that remained were stained with tobacco. Her rheumy eyes widened dramatically. She adjusted his hand and turned it right and left, examining the lines. She lifted an eyebrow and peered into his eyes as if he were a horse for sale at the market.

"You have good bones. You will be spared. The aura is very good, orange with tinges of blue. I see lions. They are not hunting. But there is death around you . . ."

The gypsy let him go and pulled Thomas toward her. She wrenched down Thomas' lip, as if to evaluate his teeth. "You are a brave boy, yes?" She pinched his cheek and let it go. "But black is near. It's on you. It's leaking. You will die."

Daniel's mother drew him back, but Thomas snickered. "What do you know, old woman?"

Mama backhanded him lightly in the chest. "Thomas! Watch yourself." Everyone knew attracting a gypsy's attention was bad enough, but to insult one?

"And the girl--" The gypsy turned and placed her hand on Camila's shoulder and drew her in. "Black is leaching into her aura, too. Death."

Daniel's mother pulled Camila away as if the gypsy's hand were death itself. The old crone turned to his mother and peered into her eyes. "You can stop this madness. There is a curse here for you." She raised her hands in the air and shook them to ward off immediate danger. "Leave this place as soon as you can."

Daniel had never seen his mother's face lose color so fast. It was white and her mouth was slightly open. "It's nothing," his mother said as she hurried them across the street. Papi's truck rumbled up. The kids got into the bed of the truck, and Mama got into the passenger seat and whispered something. Papi hit the gas, and Daniel lurched forward, then held onto the side. The last he ever saw of the old woman was in a cloud of dust.

Six months later, Thomas died in a random accident walking home from a friend's house.

Seven months after that, his sister Camila lay in a coffin, dead from a viral infection.

Within eighteen months, his father had secured a job with the embassy. Mama never went back to Argentina.

Daniel picked up his cell phone and called her. To his surprise, she answered this time.

"Daniel, I know what you are going to say. Don't speak, let me talk."

Daniel stood up from the couch. He wished to do something, shake her, hug her, anything but stand and be calm.

"I don't know exactly what is in the boxes you are requesting, but there could be something that would tarnish your father's reputation or mine for that matter."

Instead of trying to convince her, he decided to ask her something. "What would you like to do?"

"I want some guarantees."

"Like what?" he said warily.

"Like a promise that our name isn't tarnished in this witch hunt."

"There are no guarantees. I don't know what will happen."

"Do they want you to take a genetic test?"

Daniel's stomach flipped. *Why would she be asking about that?* "What are you talking about?"

"Don't play stupid with me. I know who contacted you. It's what those ladies do. The Mother's of the Plaza. They want the boxes, otherwise you would have never asked for them."

"Will the results surprise me?"

"Will you take the test? I know you want to. You were born in 1983, the last year of the war. You think your father was involved in the killings and the stealing of children, don't you?"

Why didn't she reassure him? "Mama, if he wasn't, there is no worry to give them the boxes. Or to take the genetic test."

She didn't respond. Daniel wanted to convince her to do the right thing, but if he made one sound she would shut down. This silence was what he dreaded, but in it there was hope.

"You are my only son left to me. I have only memories and pictures of your brother and sister and a heart that is broken. It will never be healed."

Another silence stilled the air between them. He was almost afraid to breathe.

She sighed heavily. "Take the test, Daniel, if you need proof of who you are."

He hung up the phone. He didn't have any proof that

his father or grandfather actually did anything wrong, and he never would. Granpapi was nearly gone, and Papi couldn't remember. The only answer he could have, the only definitive answer he had was in his blood. He needed to know. But would knowing ruin the bonds between him and his mother? He tried not to think about it. He knew the future was not written in the blood of his past.

With renewed conviction, he picked up the swab and stuck the cotton tip into his mouth. He swabbed the inside of his cheek, and then placed it in a plastic container. He put it in the pre-addressed box, walked to the post office and thrust the package into a blue bin before he could change his mind.

Chapter 9

*E*leanor was on the yellow line Metro and watching the river go by. She was on her way to Alexandria to meet Kaleb, her latest date. On Tuesday, when she had first set up the dinner using JDate, she was excited to meet him. His profile photos featured him doing adventurous things like skydiving and rock climbing. He worked as an economic advisor for the World Bank and traveled regularly. But now?

The train dipped underground, and everything went dark for a few moments before the internal lights kicked on. Eleanor barely noticed. All she could really think about was Daniel--the way he held her hips as they danced, the way he kissed her, the touch of his fingers on her breast. The train lurched and headed back up into the light. She rubbed her eyes against the sudden brightness. He was the one who wanted to help her win the game. Was he going to be just a friend? Or something more?

She checked her phone. An Instagram notification showed that Cheyenne had posted another picture. She'd scored a kiss on Tuesday with the blond from softball, and then two more on Wednesday—with two different guys at the same memorial. Eleanor shook her head. Was Cheyenne even playing the same game? Besides, two at the same place could not count toward the win. Eleanor needed to step up her game.

The Metro pulled up to her stop at the Alexandria King Street Station. The open-air platform was bustling. The buildings were sprawled out, not compact and dense like in the city. Alexandria, Virginia, was adjacent to DC. She often forgot that DC was only sixty-eight square miles with Maryland and Virginia borders. Her phone read 6:25. She was supposed to meet Kaleb at 6:30. She sat on a metal bench facing the parking lot near the bus depot to wait.

For the BINGO game, she was supposed to kiss him at the World War II Memorial. *How in the hell was she going to accomplish that?* She had tried to get him to meet her in the city, but he was adamant about Alexandria. He wanted to take her to his favorite Vietnamese restaurant for pho. She had never had pho.

And for that matter she had never been to Alexandria, even though she'd lived in DC almost six years. She shrugged. She'd find some way to get him to the monument. She scanned the crowd. No one seemed to be looking for her, but she was early.

"Excuse me, are you Eleanor?" asked a young man with dark, blondish hair and caramel-colored eyes. He had come from the Metro.

"You must be Kaleb," Eleanor said, standing to greet him.

"Yes, nice to meet you finally. I'm so glad you're here." He leaned in to give her cheek a kiss. "Ready? It's about five blocks from here."

"Sure."

They headed down King Street, and the architecture of the town changed. Gray brick buildings became slender red-brick row houses built snuggly side by side. The rectangular windows were capped with fancy white trim and wide blue shutters: a very subtle red, white and blue.

"These buildings are so tall and narrow because when they were built they were taxed on the amount of sidewalk space in front of the building," Kaleb said.

"You seem to know a lot about this."

"I studied American history. Almost majored in it. Instead I chose law school--my parents."

Eleanor nodded. She could relate to parental pressure. "I suppose you're only allowed to date a good Jewish girl?"

"Pretty much. But when I saw your picture, I had to email. You look different from the other girls, and you're in IT. I was intrigued."

Inside the pho restaurant was a largely Asian crowd. There was no host, so Eleanor and Kaleb found a table near a window. The scent of broth and soy sauce wafted through the air. Eleanor's mouth watered at the sight of bowls of clear broth filled with meat and fresh vegetables next to plates filled with basil, bean sprouts, lime and jalapeno peppers on the tables. Everyone used chopsticks. At least that part didn't make her nervous. She'd eaten at enough Chinese restaurants to know how to use them.

Kaleb waited for her to be seated first, then sat and handed her a menu that was already on the table. "My parents are from Seattle. I grew up there. Every corner had either pho or teriyaki, but back there it's a lot harder to find falafel."

"From Washington to Washington."

"I moved out here for a job. I wanted to use my law degree. This is the place to be."

The waitress came, and they ordered. Eleanor chose a vegetarian pho with tofu, and Kaleb ordered chicken pho and lotus tea.

"So why did you say yes to the date? What was it that you liked about me?" he asked earnestly.

Eleanor wasn't sure how to answer. Kaleb didn't seem to be fishing for a compliment or acting brash. He was just straightforward.

"I liked your eyes," she said, trying not to look embarrassed. The BINGO game was so dumb. Kaleb was a nice guy. She would get a kiss, but she wasn't interested in him. She didn't feel any physical connection. Logically, she should want to be with him. He was the kind of man her mother would want for her, but Eleanor didn't even want to hold his hand. "I've never seen a color like that."

Kaleb sat back, looking a little uncomfortable. Eleanor doubted herself—sometimes her directness wasn't very tactful.

"I meet most women because of my job title. I had a really awful date last week. All she could talk about was who she knew in my circles."

Eleanor maintained eye contact with him and forced a sympathetic look. "That's terrible."

Kaleb's face lightened. "I'm glad you're here because you like something about me."

The waitress returned with a large teapot and two small cups. He poured both of them a cup.

Eleanor smiled but didn't want to continue this

line of conversation. "My parents are from Poland. We came over to the States when I was twelve."

"Oh." He looked a little surprised at the abrupt change in subject. "It must be way better here," he said, arranging his napkin so that it was straight and the various sauces so they were organized.

Eleanor wasn't sure what he meant by that but decided to let it go. She didn't really care enough to ask. The plan was to get a kiss and that would be it. The conversation had been stilted so far, none of the easy companionship she'd felt with Daniel--none of the tension, the teasing. *And what was the prize Daniel kept talking about?*

"I get so nervous on first dates," Kaleb went on. "Sometimes I feel like my mother is standing right here whispering into my ear."

"That I can relate to," she said, lifting her ceramic tea cup. "To our mothers."

Kaleb raised his cup and clinked it with hers and smiled. The waitress returned to the table with two bowls of steaming pho and two plates filled with vegetables.

"Take your chopsticks," Kaleb said, placing his in his hand and snapping the air, "and add whatever you like. This is the red pepper sauce. Use it sparingly—a little goes a long way. Here's the hoisin. It's similar to soy sauce."

Eleanor loaded her bowl with bean sprouts and a few leaves of cilantro and squeezed lime over everything, but she left the sauces on the table.

As dinner wrapped up, she hinted about visiting the World War II Memorial. "You said earlier you're a big history fan. Do you want to go for a walk around the memorials?"

"I've never done that before. Sure, why not? It's a nice evening, and it's still light out. Let's get going before it gets dark." He pushed back from the table and took the bill to the cashier.

Eleanor grabbed her purse and got out her wallet to pay, but by the time she reached the front, his card had already been swiped.

They headed back to the King Street Metro, passing by Christ Church, an Episcopal church built in 1773. It was a red brick building with corners of white sandstone. The building itself was square and boxy looking, with neoclassical columns on each side of the front doors.

Kaleb pointed to the church. "George Washington used to go to this church. There's a pew inside dedicated to him. My parents and I went on a tour last year with my brother."

"That's nice." Eleanor enjoyed the information, but she was losing interest-- even friendly interest--in Kaleb. He was a talker. He filled almost every silence that fell between them. Throughout the entire walk to the Metro station and during the wait in the station and on the ride on the Yellow line and into a transfer to the Blue line, he spouted historical facts. She had never seen anyone with such a bad case of nervous talking. Any encouragement sent him on a new spate of trivia.

"Did you know that war memorial statues on horses with different poses have different meanings?"

"That's a common misconception. It's not true. Snopes."

"Did you know there's an underground tunnel system beneath Capitol Hill?"

"Yes." *I work on Capitol Hill. Did he not read my profile?*

"Did you know the MLK Memorial was made in China? Did you know there are only nine synagogues in DC? Did you know Darth Vader adorns the National Cathedral?" Did you know . . . did you know . . . did you know . . .

At the Smithsonian Station, the train stopped and so did he. Silently, they walked through the station and rode up the escalator. At ground level, the exit was located about the middle of the Mall, the park that lay between all the national museums. The Capitol building was only five or six blocks east. She'd been there several times as the stop was one of the closest metros to her office. This time of night the Mall was quiet, without the hustle bustle of tourists and workers. The World War II Memorial was about a ten-minute walk due west.

Kaleb smiled and took her hand. "I'm so glad you wanted to do this. I love it. Thank you. It's made my day."

Eleanor smiled and let her hand relax, willing herself to not yank it away. All she needed to do was get him to the WWII Memorial, chat some facts, get a kiss and say goodbye. She wished Daniel could be here now. As they crossed 14th Street and passed the Washington Memorial, Kaleb babbled on with more facts.

"Did you know the Washington Monument was built to commemorate George Washington?"

"Yes."

"Did you know it was the tallest structure until 1884?"

"No."

By the time they crossed 17th Street, they had naturally dropped hands.

Her mother might have appreciated Kaleb, but Eleanor could not. They arrived at the World War II monument and stood at the entrance. Fifty states and the U.S. territories were represented by granite columns set in an oval. The states were carved into the stone in capital letters with Times New Roman font. Inside the columns was a fountain. Eleanor snapped a picture of them and Instagrammed it, tagging her co-workers. Even though she hadn't actually kissed him yet, she would.

They walked to the pillar representing his state of Washington. "My family moved to Seattle after World War II," Kaleb said. He took her hand and then leaned in to kiss her on the cheek.

She drew back.

"Sorry, I got caught up in the moment," he said.

"Oh," she replied. "You just surprised me is all." She wasn't sure what to do or say next.

"Did you know this monument was built with mostly private funds?" he asked.

She chuckled. "No, I didn't know."

"Do you want to go for a drink?"

"It's getting kind of late, and it's Thursday. I have a long day tomorrow."

"Yeah, me too," he said. "Do you want to share an Uber?"

"No, I got it." She used the cue as an opportunity to take out her phone. They walked up to 17th Seventeenth Street and waited on the sidewalk. Her ride appeared within a few minutes. "It was great to meet you."

She got into the car, and the driver took off. Eleanor didn't look back, but she felt badly. She didn't like how things had ended, but she wasn't sure how to really end a date that she didn't want to be on.

Chapter 10

Eleanor arrived at the office early in the morning, beating the rush. She wanted to work in the quiet. It was a chance to catch up on all her busywork without being interrupted. She was working on logistics for the Vegas meeting when she suddenly realized that if she was going to Vegas, she needed two more kisses. After the date last night, though, part of her wanted to quit. She didn't like having to kiss guys only to win a game.

She stopped typing her email to reflect. But if it hadn't been for the game, she wouldn't have met Daniel. And she wanted to meet the Donohoe family. Getting the right job with Donohoe Industries would impress her mom. Better to stay focused on the goal at hand. With the deadline still a week away, there was time to win, but Cheyenne and Madeline had updated their Instagram accounts with new pictures. They were each at four now.

A text notification buzzed. It was from Jay, the programmer that Madeline's father wanted her to meet to discuss the code for her seating-chart app.

> ***Jay****: Hey, I got your number from Louis Asher re seating app. Can you meet after lunch?*
> ***Eleanor****: Does 2 work?*
> ***Jay****: Meet me at the Smithsonian Metro?*
> ***Eleanor****: Ok. Outside. What do you look like?*
> ***Jay****: Wearing a blue-and-white checkered shirt. Jeans. Baseball hat LA Dodgers.*
> ***Eleanor****: See you there.*

Opal, Lincoln's executive assistant, stormed into the office. Because Opal knew everyone and everything, her job was much more than just an assistant. She had an MBA from Harvard and worked directly with the congressman, mostly managing and filtering the hordes of data he had to contend with.

Eleanor had never seen her so upset. Usually Opal was the poster child for calm and collected. Her zen quality and persistent nature of getting shit done was well known around the office. She sat down at her computer, and logged in. Opal's fingers flew over her keyboard and then she'd stop, lift her smartphone, and click away. Back and forth she went, so intent she didn't seem to notice Cheyenne threading her way to Eleanor.

"What's wrong with our friend today?" asked Cheyenne as she sat on a corner of Eleanor's desk. "She's usually way more smiley."

"I don't know." Eleanor glanced at the closed door. "I've never seen her like this."

"We'll find out soon enough, I guess," Cheyenne said, "but it must be something bad if she's this upset."

Opal stood up with a sheaf of papers in hand. "Dammit," she said, approaching the two of them. Her jaw was set and her lips pursed. "I'll tell you what's wrong with me. I was headed to the print room to pick up some copies for a meeting, and well ..." She put her hand on her hip. "Did you guys really have to play this game? It's driving me crazy. I can't even make the final plane reservations until we know who wins. The worst of it? I can't answer Lincoln when he asks me for the hundredth time who is going. I hate lying to him."

"There's a whole week still, Opal," Cheyenne said.

"Fine. I can't change it. What's the count with everyone?"

"Madeline and Eleanor are at four. It should be over soon."

"But my job is harder now. And I'm pissed. I'm

sick of this stupid juvenile shit that goes on around here."

"It will be totally fine. Stop worrying so much," Cheyenne said, placing a hand on Opal's shoulder. "You're going to give yourself a cardiac arrest."

Opal shrugged off Cheyenne's hand. "We are on the verge of one of the biggest deals this office has ever done. I'm not going to sit by and watch you all screw it up."

Cheyenne crossed her arms, scowling. "We're not screwing up. Sit down. Tell us what's got you so upset."

Opal glared back, but then she took a deep breath and seemed to consider Cheyenne's words. Her shoulders relaxed a fraction. "I won't sit, but I will calm down. I *hate* lying to Lincoln. I promised myself I wouldn't become a yes-man. Ugh." She straightened up her spine. "As soon as there is a winner, let me know. I'll be sure to get everything wrapped up, you know, on *my* weekend--on *my* day off--and then Vegas will happen."

"You aren't the only one who works long hours." Cheyenne didn't look perturbed in the least, but Eleanor could tell she was mad.

Opal covered her mouth with one hand. "I can't. I can't even. I have to go anyway--a meeting." She grabbed a notebook and her computer bag from her desk. "Why the hell any of you want to play this game is beyond me."

Cheyenne and Eleanor glanced at each other. Eleanor wasn't sure what to do. She was shocked. Opal's abrupt departure was unnerving. Cheyenne ran her hands through her hair and pulled it up into a ponytail, loosely knotting it around itself. "No one is getting fired. Opal is just stressed. But remember, *no one* can know--not friends or family, no one. Just in case. Small town here on the Hill, and you know the old saying about loose lips and ships."

"Her anxiety is catching, but it is not good to talk about the game. I agree."

"Loose lips. I'm pretty funny, right, Eleanor?"

Eleanor arched an elegant eyebrow at her friend. "No." In truth, she was unsure what Cheyenne was talking about. Why would loose lips be funny?

"A girl can dream," Cheyenne said cheerily. "I know you love me." Her phone chimed. "Gotta go. If I don't see you, have a good weekend."

Eleanor nodded. "You too." Then her phone chimed too.

Kaleb: *I enjoyed our date. Interested in going out again? I'd love to see you.*

Almost immediately, she got another text message.

Daniel: *Tonight at 5:30. I can't wait to see
you. Perhaps dancing again?*

How did that . . .? Were Daniel's ears burning, as
the expression goes? She should try to scrounge up a
BINGO kiss before the weekend since Madeline was
out of town. But the thought of him sent Eleanor's
thoughts reeling. *The way he touched her, his lips, his
demanding kiss.*

Was she falling in love? No one remained in the
office to confer with, but Eleanor wasn't sure if she
wanted to talk to her coworkers. Cheyenne had
already gathered her things and was out the door. Opal
was gone. She shouldn't mix business with her
personal life. What she wanted was a walk. A walk to
the coffee shop for a dirty chai latte would help slow
her racing thoughts and help her figure out what the
hell to do.

THE CLOSEST CONGRESSIONAL café was busy.
Patrons were getting early lunches to go, and interns
were ordering a slew of drinks for their office. Eleanor
didn't mind. Ambient activity helped her to think, and
the busyness helped clarify her thoughts. She sat and
pulled out her phone to look over her messages. Three

men had texted her this morning: Jay, Kaleb and Daniel. The cliché saying *when it rains it pours* was certainly true at the moment. To be precise, Jay wasn't interested in her except for the software, so technically it wasn't accurate to include him in the count.

She would prefer if Kaleb didn't text. She wished he wasn't interested even if she appreciated the attention. Her mom would love him, though. Eleanor considered going out with him again for that reason, but she dismissed it immediately. Even though her mom *would* love Kaleb---after all, he *was* an economic analyst at the World Bank--Eleanor didn't want to lead him on. The proper thing to do was simply tell him she wasn't interested.

It's nothing personal ... no.

It's me, not you ... no.

I am not interested ... sounds mean.

Your conversation sucks ... definitely not.

I'm busy ... not direct.

I'm seeing someone else ... but was that technically true? Was she seeing Daniel?

When she got her chai latte, she tentatively sipped her drink. The chai was sweet on her tongue. That beat from the club popped into her mind along with the overwhelming intensity of his eyes. Her breath quickened. The way he would . . . his touch, his taste. She wanted Daniel. Kaleb was a good man, and her mother would be proud of Eleanor's selection, but he was boring. Eleanor got more excited ordering a pastrami on rye at the deli.

Be precise, like you always are. But Daniel was Catholic. Her mom would unequivocally reject him. And dating him would change the relationship between her and her mother. Was he worth the risk? Eleanor liked the feeling of freedom with him, the way he made her comfortable, how he could even get her to smile. A tingling sensation ran up the back of her neck. Daniel naked in bed, touching her, his body next to hers. She tried to brush it away, but her heart raced with the prospect.

Her phone buzzed again. It was junk mail, but it was already 1 p.m. If she hurried, she could grab a protein pack from the coffee shop for lunch and still be on time to meet Jay. After returning to her office, she finished the meal at her desk and took care of a few emails. She shut down her computer, deciding to work from home after her meeting with Jay. Katherine, her boss, was off-site. Madeline was in New York, and Lizbeth was out of the office working the Chinese delegation.

Eleanor headed out of the Cannon building and walked toward the Capitol South metro. She only had one stop to go, so she stood in the car and held on to a metal pole. She was a little giddy, thinking about a future in which she had sold the seating-chart app. What would she do with the extra money? Would she be able to quit her job and work full time?

The Metro was coming to her stop. Once outside, she found herself at the Mall. The streets were lined with tourist busses, and throngs of visitors walked from one museum to the other. Jay stood near a brown column that said Smithsonian Station. He was a hunk of a man, tall and bulky but not fat. He was a slimmer Dwayne "The Rock" but with sandy brown hair in a slightly longer buzz cut.

Once she made eye contact, he lifted his hand and smiled broadly, elevating his looks from average into handsome. "Hey, you must be Eleanor?"

"I am."

"Do you mind if we walk over to the Washington Monument while we talk? I've always wanted to see it up close, and I've been busy. Plus, I'm not here for long."

"Sure, that sounds good." They started walking down one of the wide dirt paths. On one side of her were large swaths of grass where the intramural leagues sometimes played softball. Lunchtime joggers were out taking a lap around the park, and the sound of a merry-go-round was nearby.

"I did a tour in Afghanistan a couple years back

and went to school after courtesy of the U.S. government, and it seems like something I should see."

"Oh, really?" Eleanor asked. Armed forces personnel were on her BINGO list. She shook her head. This was work. Not some casual kiss.

"Yeah, I got shot in exchange for one college education."

"Oh?" she said, the words surprising her. Most men she knew who had served in the military didn't speak of their reservations.

"The military helped me out. I'd still be stuck in North Dakota if it weren't for them."

"You're a long way from home," she said as they crossed over 14th Street and headed toward the monument. Several groups of excited elementary school kids, chatting and taking pictures along with their adult chaperones in matching shirts, pointed at the obelisk.

"That's the truth. I didn't know so many people came to visit. And the pictures don't do it justice," Jay said. The grounds were on a bit of a hill and created a vantage viewpoint to see the White House, the U.S. Capitol, and the Lincoln Memorial in one 360-degree turn.

They walked up to the monument itself, and Jay moved within an arm's length and looked straight up. "It's so much bigger than I thought, too. Up close, it's amazing. The way people built things back then was so fascinating. That's why I like coding. It's me building brick-by-brick.

"Coding never makes me sweat."

"Never?" He laughed. "Maybe you aren't doing it right?"

She gave him the slightest of smiles.

"Let's sit," he said, "and talk about your app." He led the way to a nearby bench. "It's great. The code you wrote is elegant and simple. I want to make tweaks, but only to increase options. I think Louis is serious about buying your app. Everything lines up. He owns a winery and wants to rent space for weddings, hire a planner. You'll have to talk dollars with him, but he has all the platforms to sell and market this app. If I were you, I'd ask for a percentage of sales in the contract."

"A percentage of sales?" she asked. "You can do that?"

"Sure, it's not really the norm, but it's still a contract. I think you'd make more money going into a venture with him than selling outright. It's probably not buy-a-private-plane money, but it is quit-your-job money."

"Thanks for the information," she said. "I appreciate it." The financial amount Louis had mentioned during their lunch meeting hedged her excitement.

The app wouldn't be worth millions of dollars, but what could it be worth?

"You're so pretty," Jay blurted out, "striking really." Suddenly he put his hands on the bench between them and kissed her.

She drew back, eyes-wide, mouth dropping open. She was shocked but not afraid.

"Shit," he said, "I thought, your lips, I mean—I thought you were interested."

"I was just thinking," she replied, somewhat indignantly.

"That was a seriously bad judgment call. Please accept my apology. I really thought you wanted--I thought we were hitting it off . . ." His voice trailed into silence, and they sat side-by-side on the bench.

She stared at him, then looked away. Was she giving a mixed signal? Had she leaned in, then backed away? After all, she had thought of kissing him for BINGO. On the other hand, there'd been zero connection. She concentrated on making her lips as neutral as possible. "I didn't mean to give you the wrong impression," she said after a minute of awkward silence. "Apology accepted."

"Thanks. Sorry about that, again. Not thinking sometimes. So anyway, Louis will contact you in the next week or so. He'll make an offer, and then you can counter if you don't like it. Once you hammer out all those details, you can share the source code with me, and we'll get to work refining it for all the different platforms. Do you have a lawyer or know someone who is?"

Eleanor relaxed and smiled. "A lawyer? This is DC."

"Ah, right."

Eleanor was ecstatic about the opportunity to sell her code. Especially since she hadn't planned to. And she also had her fourth kiss with a serviceman at the Washington Monument---check. She took a selfie of her and Jay and Instagrammed it. She was closer to winning than she'd ever dared to hope.

Chapter 11

After her meeting with Jay, Eleanor went home and finished working and then downed a quick salad. She was still hungry but didn't want to be full for her date with Daniel. She jumped in the shower and afterwards got dressed. She unwrapped her towel and put on her panties and bra first. She had chosen a pair of thongs and a bra that accentuated her pert breasts. She slipped on a pencil skirt to show off her long, slender legs and added a pullover silk drape shirt.

The doorbell rang. When she opened the door, Daniel held up a bouquet of maroon peonies in one hand and a bottle of red wine in the other. She could get used to this. Slung over his shoulder was a small cooler and a light blanket. He wore a pair of khaki pants and an pink shirt that contrasted well with his olive tone skin. Best of all, his curly dark hair was a barely contained wild mess she couldn't wait to run her fingers through.

He leaned back and let out a slow whistle. "Eleanor, you look stunning. Let me see you." His gaze traveled over her body with appreciation but not lewdness.

"You like?"

"I like," he said, setting down the cooler, wine and flowers. He held out his hands. "May I?"

She gave him her hand, and he twirled her slowly into his arms, ending with a kiss. His afternoon stubble was rough against her smooth skin. He smelled of patchouli and lavender, which made her think of spring. Eleanor wasn't used to such theatrics, but she loved it. Her skin warmed and tingled. She thought she might float on air if he let her go.

"I caught you. Right into my trap," he said.

Eleanor kissed him soundly. "Are you sure about that, Señor Prado?"

He caressed her cheek for a moment before his fingers traveled from her face, down the sides of her neck and under her arms. He lifted them, and she placed her hands on his shoulders as if she were about to slow dance with him. He settled his hands on her hips and gave them a little side-to-side. She closed her eyes and lifted her chin a bit, exposing soft flesh to him. Daniel kissed the base of her neck and made his way up to her earlobe with tiny licks and kisses. He whispered, "I am sure."

Eleanor didn't how she remained standing under his kisses. He stepped away but kept her steady. She gathered her wits and met his gaze.

"First a glass of wine, *galgita*. Then a concert. I have a basket packed for us."

She stepped away from the door, beckoning him. His eyes roamed over her body and back up to meet hers. The intensity of his gaze was hot, as if the heat of his yearning could burn her skin.

"I hope you like these," he said, stepping inside and handing her the flowers.

The fresh scent filled the living room. She buried her face in them, inhaling deeply. *She'd have peonies like this at her wedding someday.*

"Thank you. I love peonies. They're my favorite. I'll pour us a glass of wine."

"We cannot bring the bottle with us to the concert, but I thought it would be a good idea to have a drink before."

"Smart thinking," she said, walking through the doorway into the kitchen. She stood on tippy-toes to open a cabinet for a vase, giving Daniel a good, long view of her backside. She wasn't usually so brash, but he made her feel sexy and bold. She placed two glasses on the table and opened the wine. He pulled the cooler up to the counter. "I brought some of my favorite specialties."

"You packed me food?" It was the first time anyone had taken the time to do such a thing. All her dates had either been at a restaurant, movie or play of some sort.

"There is dark chocolate in there and my Greek neighbor's homemade baklava."

"Where are we going?"

"The Navy Yards has a free concert every weekend. We'll go and enjoy the music. It's jazz, I believe."

Eleanor held out a glass filled with wine. "This sounds like fun. I've never been."

"You've never been to The Yards? They redid the old wharf in Anacostia. It's a park now, but with restaurants and free music."

"I didn't even know it existed."

"Eleanor, *galgita* dear, there is so much for me to show you. Skiing. Samba. And now this. What could be next, do you think?"

She blushed at such a forward statement. "I suppose you'll have to show me."

"I will." He held up his glass. "*Salud.*"

"*Sto lat,*" she said, clinking his.

"Let's have a bite of chocolate first. I brought this especially for you. It's a dark chocolate that came in the diplomat's bag. It's handmade by an old man near the *estancia* where I grew up." Daniel opened the cooler and pulled out a tinfoil-covered square with a paper label. He unwrapped it, broke off a piece, and held it in front of her. She tried to take it, but he shook his head. "I'd like to feed it to you."

This was new. She opened her mouth, and he placed the chocolate on her tongue.

"It's better if you let it melt instead of chewing it."

The taste was exquisite. The right amount of milk and darkness, flavorful with a hint of salt. She closed her eyes to savor the flavor more deeply. He rubbed the back of her shoulder. Her body reacted, an intense ping in her center.

"I love watching you like this," he said.

Eleanor moaned as the chocolate melted and released its smooth, earthy richness. With that, his hands went around her ribs, and he kissed her. Their lips meshed together, and she kissed him back. Tongues darted in and out--tasting, exploring, taunting. His tongue danced against hers in a complicated movement that she instinctively understood. The taste of his mouth mixed with the chocolate was devastating.

He dipped his hand under her shirt. He cupped her right breast. "I've wanted to do this all day."

The lacy bra pressed against her. He traced the areola, and her nipple hardened against the fabric, wanting his touch. She arched her back slightly, and her breath quickened. Then his index finger trailed down over her belly button to the waistband of her skirt.

"I want to taste you. Right now. I cannot wait." A husky hunger filled his voice. "May I?"

Eleanor swallowed hard. She wasn't expecting this kind of request so soon at the start of their date. She should say no, but her body wanted him. "Yes."

With his hands around her waist, he lifted her to the counter. He gave her a quick kiss under her chin before lifting her skirt. Eleanor shifted so he could slide her panties off. He pulled up a chair and put his hands on her knees. He looked to her first before beginning. She nodded.

He pushed apart her knees to spread her legs. Then he slid his hands down her thighs, grasped her bottom, and scooted her closer to the edge of the counter. With his fingers, he deftly pulled her vaginal lips apart so she was exposed to him. She leaned back on her hands, feeling hot like she wanted to take off the rest of her clothes but unable to concentrate on anything else but his movements.

He looked up to meet her eyes. "I see how you want me." She did want him. And she felt braver somehow with his saying it.

With one finger, he circled her clit. He curved

around her opening before he glided two fingers inside. He moved his hand back and forth, cresting against the rim, firm and steady.

With a loud groan at the intense pleasure, Eleanor splayed her knees apart even further, unashamed of her need. "I want you."

He removed his fingers and grasped the undersides of her knees, bringing her toward his hungry mouth. His tongue was on her, his mouth lapping and licking her with rhythmic motion.

"Daniel, I want you. Now. I can't wait," she cried out, pressing her hips toward his mouth.

"Not yet. I want to feel you quiver against my lips. To taste you as you come."

Her core was blistering. She thought she might turn to ashes on her kitchen counter. His nose parted her, and his tongue flicked her clit. The muscles of her legs contracted, and she straightened them.

He held onto her, not letting go, his ravenous mouth taking it all. His tongue lashed against her.

Her chest heaved up and down, but she didn't want to stop. She wanted more. A tsunami started in her belly. Her stomach muscles tightened as the wave rode up her body. She gasped for air, gasped for release, until it came. She arched her back as the powerful orgasm traveled through her. She opened her mouth, letting out a resonant howl.

He leaned his head against her thigh, looking up at her as his fingers lightly teased her.

"We're not finished yet, Mr. Prado," she said, trying to catch her breath.

Daniel checked his watch, then grabbed her waist, setting her on the floor.

"We may not be finished, but we have to go, *galgita*. We are late!"

THEY ARRIVED in a cab at the Navy Yards with a few minutes to spare and managed to find a good spot to place their blanket. It was such a lovely evening, blue skies dotted with clouds. The weather was warm enough for shorts but not sweltering. Excited chatter rose from the audience, and there was a sense of fellowship in the air. In a way, the audience conveyed the same feeling it had the night she had met Daniel playing softball.

He opened up the basket and slid a wooden cutting board from its top. Using the lid as a shield, he leaned in so she couldn't see and grinned up at her.

"Sardo," he said, holding up a round of cheese. "It is much like Italian Romano but sweeter. Made from cow." He spun the cheese so she could read the label on top.

Next, he held up a slim tube of meat that looked a lot like a salami, and Eleanor's heart sank. How could she bring up this objection when he was being so sweet to prepare her food? She would wait. Maybe there was enough in that basket that she could avoid any pork without bringing it up directly.

"Bresaola," he said, placing the thinly sliced salted beef on the board next to the cheese.

Eleanor's mother would have gone apoplectic. She kept strict kosher and having cheese next to meat on the same board would have her cursing. Eleanor was not so strict with her diet. She'd never eat out if she were. Her mom didn't need to know she loved a good cheeseburger, but Eleanor drew the line at pork and shellfish. Otherwise she didn't worry so much about the dietary laws she'd been raised with.

"From the *campo* of a dear friend. Their cows are treated like rock stars. Their bresaola is as good as any you will see from Italy. They make some amazing chorizo as well, but that is pork. Am I right to not have included pork?"

Relief flooded her. She breathed easier and nodded. "Thank you. It's very thoughtful."

He laid some thinly sliced meats along the board. "This is lamb prosciutto, and this is an amazing pastrami." He opened two small containers, one after the other. "Chimichurri and *membrillo*, a kind of fruit, quince to be exact. The first is heaven with the bresaola, the second with the cheese. The *membrillo* comes from another friend. His family owns the largest quince orchard in Argentina and makes it in small batches." He layered grapes on the board and scattered almonds and olives between everything. "And, finally, a fresh baguette."

She'd never heard of bresaola or quince or chimichurri. "What is the chimichurri made of?"

"It's like a pesto with parsley, cilantro, some red wine vinegar and olive oil."

"How do we eat this?"

He sliced a piece of the baguette and layered it with bresaola and then drizzled a spoonful of the chimichurri on top. "First this."

She took a bite and closed her eyes, enjoying the flavors. They were unusual but delicious. The musty sweet flavors of the cheese mingled well with the bright herbs in the sauce. Eating helped to take her mind off him. She wanted nothing more than to take him home and get naked, but this tension, this waiting was worth it.

He continued to prepare her bits of food, bringing olives and almonds to her lips one at a time.

The music started, an easy beat that soothed her and provided an ethereal soundtrack to their rustic meal. He handed her a piece of cheese smeared with the *membrillo*. The salty flavor of the cheese melded with the tart quince paste into something greater than either of them.

Daniel was watching with a goofy grin.

"What?"

"I love to watch you when you are happy," he replied. "I'm going to get something to drink. Would you like wine or beer?"

"Something red," she replied.

After he left, she lay propped on an elbow on the blanket. The concert music was relaxing. She closed her eyes, and the memory of the feel of his mouth on her overwhelmed her senses. What he had done at the house, she had never experienced to that degree. Her body reacted, her skin so sensitive she was aware of a light breeze in the air. The taste of the delicious food was still on her tongue. He was coming back, and there would be more this evening. For her, it was a perfect moment.

"I'm back," he said, kneeling and handing her a clear plastic glass. "I got lucky. The line was short."

She sat up and took the glass.

"How is the game going?" he asked, his expression innocently amiable.

"I think I'm going to sell my seating-chart app," she said. "I met with a guy named Jay today, but ... it was kind of weird."

"Here, hold on to my glass." He rearranged his seating and straightened out his legs on the blanket. "Please, go on." He held out his hand for the wine.

"Jay had always wanted to see the Washington Monument, so we walked there." She hesitated, watching his expression. "It was supposed to be a business meeting. But then he kissed me."

Daniel straightened his back, and his eyes darkened for a bit, and then he relaxed. "This is for your game, right?"

"Yes, the BINGO game."

"Was this a serious kiss? Was it passionate?" He took a drink of his wine and swallowed heavily.

"No, just a misunderstanding. He thought I wanted a kiss and kissed me. It was a business meeting, but ... I don't know. It was awkward. He apologized after like a total gentleman."

"What luck for you, eh? That makes three kisses, no?"

"Four. I kissed my Jdate, too. The guy I met yesterday from the dating website. I need one more." Eleanor rubbed the edge of her plastic cup.

"Come," he said, patting his thighs, "rest here. You'll be more comfortable."

She moved until her head was on his thighs. He picked up a cluster of grapes from the cooler and plucked one off. He placed it gently on her lips. She took the grape in her mouth and bit down, sweet juice popping on her tongue. His eyes never left hers, and he pulled off another grape. She nodded, and he placed it in her mouth. She crunched the grape and swallowed.

He swept away a few strands of hair. She glanced toward the stage where the group had switched to an upbeat jazz number. In the audience, some people had stood and were dancing to the music, while others were animatedly talking with friends. Lots of couples, though, were sitting close to each other, quiet like her and Daniel, having a romantic evening. Relaxed and free, she tapped her toes to the music. A breeze warmed her skin and brought with it the earthy smells of the water. If she could, she'd make this moment last forever.

The concert ended as the sun was beginning to set. The night was young. Crowds moved out of the Navy Yard, buzzing with Friday night excitement. Eleanor watched as a mother picked up her tired daughter and held her. What had it been like for her mom all those years as a single parent? Eleanor knew only from a child's perspective. A sense of appreciation came over her as she realized all her mother had done for her. But she wondered what her future family would look like. Would she have a standard Jewish family? She couldn't picture that, either.

Daniel put the leftover food into the cooler. He took her hand and helped her up.

"What do you want to do now? The night's still early. But we have the cooler. It's not something I want to carry around. Let's go back to your place first, and then go from there."

She nodded. The suggestion of going back to her place made her want to run there. Daniel led her toward the exit. Words were not necessary.

The humid air cooled and caressed her skin like a lover. It was as though she was walking through bliss. They got into a cab, and she gave the driver her address. Daniel held her hand close against his stomach, his own fingers curled around hers. He rubbed her fingers, bringing them to his mouth, kissing their tips and knuckles, his eyes intent on hers. He snuck a pass at the edge of her breast; her hand rested on his upper thighs. Eleanor leaned in as if to whisper something, but instead of words she exhaled warm breath into his ear and licked the inner curve of his lobe.

By the time they got to her block, they were both exhaling light, uneven breaths. They separated for a moment to get out of the cab and pay. It had dropped them off at the wrong spot a few houses away. Eleanor stood with a hand on her hip and a naughty grin. "Catch me if you can!" she taunted before sprinting off. *Had she lost her mind?*

"Not fair." Daniel sprang after her, one arm wrapped around the cooler.

Eleanor ran as hard as she could for home. She managed to unlock the door and dash inside. He was right behind her, dropping the cooler in the entry. Breathing heavily, he shut the door with a foot and lunged for her, grabbing her around the waist and swinging her around. He picked her up, and she wrapped her legs around his waist---her arms around his neck. He kissed her throat with small, tiny kisses that sent ripples up her spine.

"Well, Mr. Prado. You caught me."

"And what should I do with you now?"

She squeezed her thighs around him. He leaned her back against the wall. Holding onto him with one hand, she slid her hand between them to find his cock. *She needed him to take her.* He grunted, voice cracking with want. She tried to undo his pants, but she couldn't find the button between them.

"My prize," he said, leaning against her, smashing her with his desire, pinning her against the wall. He kissed her. Gentle at first, a nibble, and then parting her lips, his tongue demanding entry. He pulled her shirt down and squeezed her breast under her translucent bra, pinching her nipple, twirling it in his fingers.

He held Eleanor under her butt and lifted her away from the wall. She tightened her grasp around him. His dick was throbbing and hard against her pussy. Daniel carried her to the stairs and up to her bedroom. They collapsed together on the bed. His breath ragged, he took off her shirt and let it fall to the floor. She lifted her hips to him, and he slid off the skirt, leaving her bra and underwear.

He stood and removed his khakis and button-down. Then he pushed her legs apart and kneeled on the bed between them. He palmed her breasts and pulled down the bra. His mouth came down hard on her. His tongue found her nipple and he sucked and gently bit it until it was hard as quartz. His mouth left her breast, and he kissed the space between, raining small pecks down to her belly button. She arched back and pulled her knees apart to give him access--his need, his embrace, driving her own desire. He kissed her legs on either side and caressed her inner thighs with an insistent measure.

His head lowered. He nibbled at her clit through her underwear, unable to get a firm grip on her, driving her mad. She cried out in pleasure, clutching at his hair and running her fingers through his silky-soft curls. Her clit was swollen, still aching for his touch.

He turned her over so she was on her stomach and then lifted her hips to him, her ass high in the air. Alternating between small kisses and little licks, he followed the edge of her thong between her ass cheeks until he reached her clit.

"Your taste," he said, caressing her lower back. "I love it."

The way he said it--the throaty tone, the accent--excited her. Eleanor wanted more. He had unleashed a side to her she didn't know existed. With her hands on the headboard, she pushed herself into him. "I need you inside me," she gasped. "Now."

He didn't answer, instead exhaling warm breath on her pussy. The tickling air against her throbbing clit almost made her come.

"Wait for me," he said. "I'll be right back." Like that, he was gone. Eleanor sat up. She heard him thump down the stairs to the kitchen.

When he returned, he held a peony in his hand. "Take off your bra and underwear."

She did as he requested, tossing the garments to the side.

"Lay back and close your eyes," he commanded.

Unsure of what he had planned, she lay down cautiously and shut her eyes. A slight breeze came into the room, swishing the curtains. He let the petals whisper against the base of her neck and collarbone. He whisked the flower over her nipples, circling them with the blossom. The delicate touch caused her skin to ripple with goose bumps.

"Your body is so beautiful," he said. With the base of his palm, he rubbed the top of her nipple, and it rose into a hard bud. A fresh wetness covered her labia. Her clit pulsed, starved for him.

"You," he said, tracing the flower down her abdomen and making a circle around her belly button. He continued down and over her mound. He kneeled between her legs as she spread them wide, welcoming him, every inch of her body alive. The petals fluttered across the top of her pussy, softening the bloom with her juices.

"Open your eyes." He brought the flower up to his nose and inhaled deeply. "I love the way it smells."

She dug her hands into the bed. He pulled the petals off the flower and scattered them on her, tossing the stem to the floor. The heady scent of the flower mixed with the smell of sex.

He was on his knees between her thighs. "Someday we won't need this. But for now, yes?" He ripped the condom package open, and she watched him roll the condom on.

"Wider, *mi galgita*," he said, catching his breath.

She did as he asked, laying her knees on the bed, excited with the anticipation of having him inside her. She felt so exposed, so vulnerable, so free to him. *Someday*—the word promised so much more than a single night of passion.

"Use your fingers to open yourself," he said. His breathing was ragged but in control.

She played herself open as he bid and dipped a finger inside. A low growl came from him.

He pushed the tip of his penis into her and circled his hips again, the tip rounding her opening out. "I love the feel of you, Eleanor, you are so hot and wet."

She lifted her hips to him, inviting him in, begging silently. He lowered himself slowly inside. Instead of coming straight down, he rounded his hips again, widening her, readying her for what was to come. Her hips twitched, and she scraped her nails down his shoulders and arms. All she wanted was for him to plunge inside, to satisfy this tortuous anticipation, to quell her need.

He filled her hard, going deep, touching her secret place. He marked her like no one else. He reached her core, the essence of her. He thrust into her. She met his rhythm, squeezing the muscles of her vagina tight around his cock.

She opened her eyes and watched as his throbbing dick disappeared into her, shiny with their juices. The sight of it caused her clit to throb, and she reached down to touch herself. Daniel's eyes flew open. They were dark with pure adrenaline and carnal lust. Knowing she did that to him boosted her confidence. She rubbed her clit in time with him and could feel the back of his dick as it plunged in and out of her.

Her orgasm was coming. Her core swelled, and she squeezed her thighs as hard as she could to brace for the oncoming surge. His rhythm changed, faster, pummeling her center with an animalistic pulse. He closed his eyes and lifted his head, pounding into her as if nothing else mattered. His legs stiffened, and there was one final thrust. His hot cock throbbed inside her, spasm after spasm.

He collapsed onto her. Their breath was ragged but caught up together in the same inhale and exhale rhythm.

Daniel rolled off her and sank onto the bed. "Come here you," he said, pulling her closer.

She snuggled into his arms, and he kissed her gently. Arms and legs intertwined with each other, unable to tell where she stopped and he began.

"My god, *galgita*. You are incredible." He kissed her on the lips, on her cheek, until she felt unconditionally loved, as if he had taken her back to a simpler time.

"I don't think I'll ever be able to move again," she said, smiling between the kisses. "I'm hungry now. How about you?"

Daniel put his boxers back on. "Let's order

Chinese. I'll call from my phone." He smiled and left the room.

"Orange chicken and lettuce wraps," she called, knowing what she wanted. "I'll be but a minute." She opened a drawer to get a clean pair of panties and put on a robe.

"Where's the number for Chinese?" he hollered.

"On the fridge. I'll be in the living room," she said. "Come out and snuggle with me."

A minute or two later, he came in with a glass of water and sat on the couch. Soon, they had picked out a movie and were cuddled on the couch together with a blanket thrown over them. It was as if they had known each other forever. The doorbell rang, and Eleanor paused the show to collect the food.

They sat crossed-legged on the couch, taking turns passing the little waxed boxes back and forth. When she thought of their actions only a short while ago--how she was so exposed and the insane pleasure that had come with it--she sighed and smiled.

Daniel glanced up at her and then away. "I want to tell you something. It's probably not a big deal."

His expression sent shivers of anxiety through her. "You can tell me," she said, not sure she really wanted to know. "It sounds important."

His brown eyes connected with hers. They were somber, without their usual mirth. "I'm trying to convince my mother to release some boxes that my father had saved."

"Just some boxes? What's in them that's so bad?"

"My father worked for the military after the Argentina junta took power." Daniel paused to finish a bite and pointed his chopsticks in the air. "I love him, but I don't think he is the man that I knew."

"I read about the junta a long time ago. Something along the lines that the military took over the country. But what happened with your dad? What did he do that was so bad?"

Daniel wouldn't look at her. He took another bite of his food, chewing slowly, and she assumed he was contemplating his next words.

She curled her legs under her and hesitated before she spoke. "My mom won't go back to Poland, either. World War II was terrible, but it seemed like Poland took longer to recover than other countries. My grandmother, she was like a stone. And the pogroms that came later... so much pain. My aunt and uncle were killed in the early '80s during a pogrom. I didn't know them, but my mom cries whenever she thinks of them. In the '80s--that's not so long ago. It's insane to me that this still happens in our modern world. And when my dad died, it was like she lost the last bit of heart she had."

Daniel had leaned back and cocked his head,

listening. His eyes conveyed empathy, but his scrunched-up shoulders indicated he was not entirely comfortable with the conversation at hand.

"I tell you this because I understand a hard life," Eleanor said. "I understand family relationships are difficult."

He shrugged as if he'd come to an internal decision. "I know you do. That is why I am telling you. Since I met you, I have felt braver. That my job is to do the right thing. These boxes I am telling you about may have information that could help a group of people, but in giving the boxes away, it may implicate my father in wrongdoing." Daniel looked behind him toward the door as if he might escape, but he ground his teeth. "It doesn't matter. My mama must live her life, right?"

"Yes, it does matter." Eleanor placed a finger on his chin and turned his face to hers. "There is more to a home than a location." She lifted the pendant he wore around his neck and cupped it in her palm. Its weight was comforting, and she suddenly understood why he might wear it all the time. "Remind your mother of this."

His arms went around her, and he scooped her onto his lap. He rested his head between her breasts. She felt him give a slight shudder and pulled him in closer. She kissed him on the forehead and ran her fingers through his hair in a soothing way, lightly from the nape of his neck to his scalp. His arms tightened, and he emitted a deep sigh. They sat together, quiet, wrapped in each other's arms.

She couldn't remember how it happened, but he carried her to bed. He took off her T-shirt and panties, telling her he needed to be naked so every part of her body was touching his. Their faces were close, noses touching, and he rubbed her cheeks with his scratchy ones. He opened his eyes, watching her, telling her something with no words. His hands smoothed down her back and over the curve of her waist, cupping her butt and bringing her toward him as if she were the most precious thing--as if he were claiming her. She trusted him and relaxed. She massaged his shoulders. Exhaustion from the week settled her even further, and soon they were both asleep nestled into each another.

Chapter 12

*E*leanor woke to the image of Daniel's face--sweet and innocent looking. He emitted a tiny snore as he breathed in and out. She kissed him on the nose, then untangled herself. It was the weekend, and she didn't have to work. In the kitchen, she started the coffee machine. Then she opened the refrigerator and considered the contents. There was orange juice and a few leftover bialys that her mother had made, leftover latkes, a couple to-go containers, a half-dozen eggs, yogurt, and a variety of condiments. She pulled out the bialys to toast and turned to place them on the counter. Daniel stood in the doorway to her kitchen stark naked. She looked down at his penis. There was a lot of skin wrinkled at the tip. She had only seen a few dicks before, but it didn't look like a normal penis.

There wasn't the helmet or the head or whatever it was called.

"Can I get a cup? For my coffee?" he asked nonchalantly.

"Coffee? Er, let me . . ." Unable to resist, she examined him again. She widened her eyes in an effort to see more clearly. "What? I mean, what is that?" She gestured to his penis.

"What do you mean?" he asked, grinning from ear to ear.

"What's wrong with it?"

His eyes held an expression of amusement. "Did you find something wrong last night?"

"No," she said. Her face felt hot at the reminder of their nocturnal activities. "That's not what I meant. It's different."

"I'm not circumcised. This is an uncut penis, *mi galgita.*" He lifted it up so she could see it clearly and pulled back the foreskin. "Does this look more like what you are used to?"

Eleanor swallowed suddenly like something had caught in her throat. She hadn't expected him to be so forthcoming. "Yes, well--okay. That is what I have seen before. Is it unclean?"

"You are direct. Anyone ever tell you that?"

"Well? That is why it is cut, to keep it clean."

"I keep it very clean. I wash it thoroughly every day. You don't need circumcision for that."

"Do you feel . . . less or more?"

"I don't know how to answer that question," he said, approaching her and smiling slyly. "But everything feels good. Research shows that a man has more sensitivity with it uncut, but I've heard the same from a cut man."

"Oh." She was unsure what to say. He closed the small amount of distance between them until they stood toe to toe. His hands slid from her shoulders, down her back, and he dug his fingers into the thickness of her bottom. "Want to go again? In the name of research, yes?"

"We eat first." She pushed him back with an "as-if" grin, but her body reacted instantly with a wetness that covered her sensitive labia. Feeling naughty, she spread her legs and leaned down to open the refrigerator to get some yogurt. She pulled aside her panties to give him a good look at her wet pussy. Without hesitating, he shut the fridge door and moved behind her. He placed his hands on her waist and shifted her over a few steps, so she was leaning over the counter. Eleanor propped herself on her elbows. Leaving her thong on, he pulled her vaginal lips apart.

"Get a condom," she gasped.

"I only had one."

"I'll get one from upstairs."

"Hurry." His finger stole down her damp slit. "Get a pair of shoes, too. High heels."

Eleanor turned. "High heels?"

"Yes," he said with a nod.

She scampered to her room and dug through her bedside table for a condom. The last time she'd used one of them had been so long ago she hoped it wasn't expired. Then she found her most expensive four-inch-high Louboutin's, black with red soles, set on a shelf in her closet waiting for a special occasion. This was going to be special, of that she was certain. She popped them on and took off her t-shirt. She sauntered down the hallway, covering her breasts, but feeling sexy in only her underwear.

He gave her a low whistle when she strutted back into the kitchen.

"Come to me," he said. She walked into his arms. He embraced her first, wrapping his arms around her waist and smelling her hair. "I promise you will like this," he whispered into her ear.

With her nod, he turned her and ran his hand along her spine. She leaned over the counter and stepped wide, handing him the condom over her shoulder. He pulled down the thong to her upper thighs. The underwear kept her legs relatively close, and with the high heels, her hips were raised into the air. His hand rested warm on her lower back. With his other hand, he slipped first one finger inside and then two, pulsing against her G-spot. She groaned and pressed back, wanting him, the entrance of her opening still sensitive from last night.

"You're perfect," he said. As he removed his fingers, he dragged them over her ass. The tip of his hard dick circled her clit. He slid himself in slowly, the wonderful, aching pressure stretching open. She tightened every muscle and squeezed herself, as if bonding herself to him.

"You're so tight, my little *galgita*."

Eleanor pressed her body as flat as she could against the countertop and lifted her hips higher to let him in deeper. Her nipples were hot against the cold tile. He grasped the sides of her hips and pulled her to him, his broad length fully inside. The palms of his hands slid up her back until he was leaning over her. He hooked his hands into the crooks of her elbows and lifted. Eleanor's back arched until only her nipples touched the counter. The pressure within was exquisite.

He swung his hips to the side and with a circular movement plunged into her. She screamed out in pleasure, unable to restrain herself. He built up a rhythm with his pounding, grunting as if he were a wild animal. His rock-hard dick was unforgiving in her body, touching places she had never felt before. Pleasure flared through her, up her spine and down her legs. Her body clenched onto him, and a climax came from her belly and out her mouth in breathy, uncontrolled gasps. He stiffened, and she felt his final thrust.

Slowly, he withdrew. He brought her into his arms for a tight embrace, his whole body against hers. "Let me make you breakfast," he said with a kiss on her nose. "I want to take care of you."

She smiled at him, surprised. Her sore and tired body relaxed into his arms. She laid her head on his shoulder and traced her fingers around the blades of his shoulder. "I'd like that. I have to go to the bathroom. I'll be right back." She paused at the kitchen doorway. "I have never had anyone make me breakfast. I don't have much food."

"I'll figure something out."

In the bathroom, she took off her shoes, then splashed water on her face. Her legs were cold, so she put on a pair of pajama bottoms and an old T-shirt. Her shaky thighs made her feel as if she'd just run a marathon. The smell of eggs cooking floated in. *He really cooks?* She brushed her hair and, on her way, out grabbed a robe for Daniel.

In the kitchen, three pans were on the stove top. In one, the latkes sizzled. In another, he'd heated up lamb and grilled red peppers from one of the to-go containers that had Mediterranean food, and in the third, eggs were frying. On each plate lay a toasted and buttered bialy. Two cups of coffee steamed on the counter.

"What is this?" she asked, dubious. Her mother did not consider cooking skills as part of the criteria for a possible husband. But Eleanor loved it. She handed Daniel the pink and frilly robe.

"This is yours?" he asked, holding it out to the side. "I guess I expected something . . . different, functional, I guess." He took her hand and kissed her wrist. "Thank you." He wrapped the girly robe around his powerful shoulders and tied its silky sash in a bow. "I wasn't sure if you took cream or sugar," he said, pointing to the coffee.

"I like it black, actually, so it's perfect. What are you making? Do you know what you're doing?" she asked, not that she could detect any deficiency in his culinary skills. She had never had a man in the kitchen getting his hands greasy for her. He selected a plate and slid out a latke, topped it with the leftover lamb and grilled peppers, then capped it with an over-easy egg. He stuck a fork in the egg, and the yolk ran over the edges.

Eleanor leaned and inhaled. The smell of eggs and the latkes reminded her of growing up in Poland. He put the pans into the sink and ran some water and added soap.

Daniel and Eleanor heard the front door swing open, but they were unable to see who it was. He grabbed a wooden spoon and moved Eleanor so that she was behind him.

"Eleanor? Are you ready?" asked a woman's voice.

The only person who had a key was ... *please, let it be a burglar. A female thief who dared to break in during the middle of the morning. Anyone but ...*

"What is this mess out here? Eleanor? Eleanor!"

... *her mom.* She was standing in the doorway staring at Daniel. A shriek erupted through the air. Eleanor's mother dropped a loaf of challah. It bounced on the floor with a thud. No one moved to pick it up. She had on a conservative dress with a matching pillbox hat to wear to the synagogue, her gray hair pinned securely. Her mouth had settled into a comical O. She was looking at Daniel. Her eyes dropped.

The tie to Daniel's pink and frilly robe had loosened during his cooking. His entire torso, Catholic penis and all, was completely on display.

"Whoa!" Daniel said, his surprise making his accent thick. He put the wooden stick down and pulled the robe together, knotting the tie. "Pleased to meet you, ma'am. I am at your service."

Eleanor bit her lip and exhaled slowly. At least her

mother hadn't shown up five minutes ago. She shut her eyes and rubbed her face. *Usually* her mother called first to confirm if they were attending Shabbat together. *Usually* her mother would call before she came over, but Eleanor wasn't surprised. It was like her mom to show up unannounced and let herself in the door. But of all the days to do that, why this one?

Her mother's hands moved to her hips, and she wore a glare that would stop the Almighty himself. "I'm her mother," she said in an imperious tone. "Who the hell are you?"

"My name is Daniel Prado," he said, his shoulders squared. He gave Eleanor a how-was-I-supposed-to-know look and smiled broadly.

"Mom, I--You're supposed to call me first? Remember?"

"Is this why? So you can . . ." She left the sentence unfinished and glowered. "Eleanor? What is the meaning of this? Are you coming with me to the synagogue?"

Eleanor glanced sheepishly back at Daniel. He had relaxed his stance and picked up his cup of coffee. The combined task of getting him dressed and out the door, getting herself ready, walking to temple and being on time was overwhelming. More important, she didn't want to. A gorgeous Argentinian man had just made her a delicious breakfast. She wanted to stay home, eat food and do--other things. A rebellious feeling rose inside her.

"I'll be there next week. I promise."

"I am not leaving. Aren't you going to even introduce us properly?" her mother asked, straightening her back and adjusting her buttoned jacket.

"Mom." Eleanor picked up the challah bread and tried to hand it back to her.

"Please introduce us, Eleanor," she said, pointedly ignoring the bread.

"As he just told you, this is Daniel Prado. Daniel, this is my mother, Mrs. Rebekah Winslow."

"It's a pleasure, ma'am," he said, coming toward her with his hand extended as if to shake hands. Mrs. Rebekah Winslow gave him a withering look. He stopped and gave her a stiff bow.

Eleanor thought her mother looked as calm as the sea, but when her mother didn't move a muscle, that was the time to run.

"Daniel Prado, the pleasure is *not* mine."

"Mom," Eleanor said, trying not to sound embarrassed or whiny but definitive and strong. She tried to steer her mother toward the door.

"Not yet, dear. Daniel, would you pour me a cup of coffee, please?"

Daniel did as he was told even though he was half

naked. He poured a fresh cup of coffee and handed it to her.

"Ah, thank you. I take it black." Rebekah took the cup from him but remained standing. "Daniel, where are you from?"

"Buenos Aires, ma'am. Baradero to be exact."

"Please do call me Mrs. Winslow. I would appreciate it more than ma'am."

Daniel smiled at her charmingly, his dimples on overdrive. "Of course, Mrs. Winslow."

"Now, Daniel, what is it you do for a living?"

"I work for the Embassy of Argentina."

"That sounds lovely indeed. And how did you meet my daughter?"

"We played a game of softball."

Thankfully he did not add *this week*. Eleanor watched the mini tête-a-tête with growing foreboding. Her mother was too calm, asking questions as if she were at a cocktail party, not in Eleanor's kitchen with a half-naked man.

The silence that hung in the air was a living thing. It seemed it could reach out and capture Eleanor or Daniel if they spoke, so they remained quiet.

"Feh. Fine." Rebekah picked up a piece of bialy from one of their plates and held it out toward Eleanor. "This is from a recipe your grandmother taught me."

Eleanor knew exactly what she meant by that. Her

mother was upset about finding her with a man, but not only that, her mom knew Daniel was not Jewish. She'd seen him naked. That's really all it took.

"Thank you for a lovely breakfast," Rebekah said, taking the piece of bread with her. "I'll show myself to the door. No need to meet up later."

Eleanor went to give her mother a hug but changed her mind when she saw her expression. "I'm sorry, Mom. I'll call you later."

Mrs. Winslow put up her hand and walked out. Eleanor leaned against the kitchen doorway, watching her mother leave through the front door. She could almost feel the glare through the solid wood. After calming herself, she returned to Daniel.

"Your mom reminds me of my own mother." He stared at the bright red lipstick stains on Rebekah's coffee cup.

Eleanor said nothing. She took the cup off the counter and put it in the sink. Unable to leave it be, she turned on the water and washed it.

"*Galgita* darling, don't worry. Your mom will come around. Enjoy your meal," he said, pushing the plate toward her. "Or do you want me to go?"

She didn't want him to go but couldn't face him. Instead, she focused on the bread. A ripple of anger ran through her body. When was she going to act like an adult? She was twenty-four years old. If she wanted to have sex, damn it, she was going to have sex. Daniel was right. Damned if she was going to let her mother ruin her morning. But when she looked up, he was gone. She ran into the living room where he was putting on his pants.

"Daniel, I want you to stay."

"I'd be obliged." He placed a hand behind her neck. She leaned into it as he kissed her. She could taste the coffee and peppers. He led her to the bedroom. She got another condom out first, then pushed him down in the bed. She got on top of him. She wanted to feel free, liberated. Her hips rolled back and forth over him until she came, quietly and fiercely.

Chapter 13

On Saturday afternoon, Eleanor and Daniel went for a walk and on the way back grabbed some falafel from a street vendor. When Daniel finally left, she didn't want him to go. But he had prior plans for the evening, an event at the embassy. He said he would have invited her, but the ambassador was speaking and the guest list cemented. He would call later.

For the first time in four days, Eleanor was by herself. She wanted a nice hot bath, Thai food delivered and a movie on Netflix. She had just stripped when the phone rang. Her mother appeared on the smart phone. Eleanor answered the call without video.

"Hi, Mother." Eleanor held the phone with her shoulder as she grabbed for her pink robe. It still smelled wonderfully of Daniel.

"What are you doing? Your voice sounds different."

"I don't sound any different."

"Is he there?"

"No," Eleanor said, tying the sash around her waist. "Mom, I'm not marrying the guy. We had a date."

"Well, it's too late for a date, isn't it? Haven't you already ... kissed?"

"Mother!" The memories of what she had done less than twenty-four hours ago made Eleanor's face hot. "It was just a date," she stammered. *Why did her mother always reduce her to feeling like a child who had been caught with a hand in the cookie jar?*

"Don't you remember where we came from? We didn't have much in Poland. We were poor."

The statement came as a bit of a surprise to Eleanor. She had always had friends to play with, and what she wore didn't seem to matter. She didn't remember her childhood as being poor. They were never hungry that she remembered. It was always homemade, even if it wasn't the best quality. Her mother hadn't changed until after Tutti had died, when she seemed to have a remark for everything that was different in the US.

"Yes, I remember Poland. It wasn't that bad," Eleanor replied. "I don't remember being poor."

"That's because you were a child. You didn't have to worry about where your next meal would come from. I did that for you."

The desire to hang up on her mother was strong. The truth was, even if they were poor, it was no longer their truth. But Eleanor didn't know how to express that sentiment to her mother. She seemed determined to live in the past.

"To avoid being poor, you must also marry well. You'll do good to remember there is no one in your future but a good Jewish boy."

"Daniel and I just met. I'm not going to marry him," Eleanor said. "He is a good man. He's trying to help—"

"It doesn't matter," replied her mother, cutting her off.

Eleanor clenched her teeth. She was tired of the disparaging conversation, but it was easier to let her mother rant than it was to correct her.

"You must have same religion, same background. Otherwise it is too hard. Marriage is more than silly feelings of love. Your father and I didn't know each other when we got married. We were strangers. It was arranged. I was scared, but I did the right thing. I grew to love him."

"Okay, mother. I'll keep that in mind," Eleanor said quietly. She knew this was an indirect way of instructing her that Daniel was not Jewish and that he would drag her down.

"I married Jewish so all the important questions were answered. The kind of questions that don't seem important until it is too late. Especially those that come up while you are raising children."

"I wish Tutti was still here. I miss how he played for us. He played the mandolin, right? Or was it a guitar?"

"The mandolin. The man was a genius on it. He used to serenade me after we were betrothed."

"That's sweet." Eleanor didn't listen to that kind of music anymore, not since his death. Usually after dinner he'd play sweet and slow songs. Sometimes, on a Friday night he'd play a polka, and she and her mother would dance in the living room. After Tutti died, she and her mother had clung to each other with tears and sorrow in a new country, a new land. But now that clinging felt claustrophobic.

"You're right, Mom. I shouldn't date anyone but good Jewish boys." Eleanor didn't really believe that. For a long time she had believed, but more often than not she dated Jewish guys to appease her mom. She studied her reflection in the mirror. Her skin had a gleam to it. She was clean and living in a nice town-home. Her teeth were straight and white thanks to modern dentistry. She didn't want to relive the old memories. She felt good.

"I want you to do me a favor."

"What is it?" Eleanor pinned her short hair back with a bobby pin. "What do you need?"

"You to go out with Abraham, the son of Mrs. Stein's cousin."

"What? Mother, there's no way I am going on a date with this Abraham."

"Are you going to be with Daniel? A Catholic?" her mother asked. "Is that what I tell Mrs. Stein?"

"No. Ugh. Fine."

"I saw her this morning, and she was telling me all about Abe. He's an accountant and would be a good match for the family."

"Mother, I have plans."

"If they are with Daniel, cancel them. It's better you do it now, before you must break up with him anyway. Besides, I had to offer a special favor to Mrs. Stein. I promised her my recipe for the bialys."

Wait. Did her mother say she had to bribe Mrs. Stein? Eleanor caught her reflection in the mirror. Why would her mother act like she should be traded for two sheep and a goat? She wasn't some kind of commodity.

A notification pinged her phone. One of the girls had posted a picture on Instagram and scored another letter for BINGO. In spite of how she felt about Daniel, maybe a date with Abe wouldn't be a bust. "What kind of job does he have?" she asked.

"Oh? You are starting to finally care about their job titles? That's a good sign. He works for the IRS."

Yes. He qualified as a BINGO kiss. *A kiss that would win the game. Oy vey!* First Daniel, then Kaleb, next Jay--and now her mom wanted to set her up on a date. Men were popping up on the radar. Some days she believed people operated more like networked systems than independent code.

"Is Daniel there?" her mother asked. "Never mind. I don't want to know. You have a date."

Eleanor caved. A date cost a couple of hours of her time. If she didn't, she'd never hear the end of it, and it would be worth it to get her mother off her back.

"All right, Mom. I'll go out with Abraham."

Eleanor didn't know how to be strong with her mother. She understood her mom only wanted the best for her, but it always ended up being what her mother *thought* was the best, not necessarily what Eleanor wanted. Until she married, she'd be a child in her mother's eyes.

Chapter 14

On Sunday, Daniel did not have plans to go see his mama, but after spending Saturday with Eleanor he knew what he had to do about his family. He wouldn't steal the boxes. He wouldn't take them without her permission. Marietta Prado could not serve two masters, and an accounting was due. He wanted to remind Mama that home was where they made it; he was her home as well. The message had to be wrapped in love and understanding. If he used any sort of threat against her, she would shut down and cut him off.

Years ago, he had wanted to go home to see Granpapi, and Mama staunchly refused. Daniel, being twenty-two, could have gone on his own, but he felt that she needed to be with him. She refused, and he had responded with yells and passionate cajoling and became so angry he struck the wall, leaving a hole in the drywall. After that, she had shut down. They didn't speak to each other for six months. His loss of control had scared him, and he promised himself to never react with physical anger again. It had been difficult, but he had kept his promise since that day.

He went alone to see his grandfather and hated himself for it. During that time, the *estancia* felt like a place he used to go to but had forgotten. His home wasn't the same as it was in his memories. Daniel realized that while he cherished his granpapi and loved his father, it was an adoration veiled with the unmarred love of a child. Back then, both men were bigger than life and could do no wrong.

His mother had been the real parent over the years. She was the one who disciplined him, the one who kissed his bruises to make the tears stop, the one who had tucked him in at night, the one who made him breakfast every morning. He would not hurt her. He would not force her to do anything. He would not put their relationship in jeopardy over the Grandmothers of the Plaza.

But the past was beginning to create new rot.

He cruised down Lee Jackson Memorial in his friend's car, a BMW M4 GTS. Daniel loved the manual shift as the car accelerated down the highway. He turned into the long driveway to Mama's house around 11:30 a.m. A few horses were idly eating grass in the front pasture, but her favorite horse was not among them. Early church service ended around 9:30. If she went riding afterwards, she was usually back by noon. He reconsidered the idea of removing the boxes without her knowledge to avoid a confrontation. There was enough time to move the boxes and head back to DC without her knowing it. He parked the car in front of the house.

The wide cement path to the barn was lined with poppies in full bloom and sporadic Japanese maples. The stall doors were open and the horses outside in the pasture. He walked straight to the old tack room. One side of the room held wooden saddle racks covered with sheepskin. He pulled back the country-plaid curtains on the small window to let some light in. His old saddle was still in Argentina. Someday he hoped to collect it. Worn horse blankets were neatly folded on a shelf. The boxes were shoved into a corner. A dusty blanket lay on top of them. He removed it and shook it. The room turned hazy as the light hit the clouds of fine dust and hay.

The boxes were Papi's old work cartons. Daniel wasn't even sure if they held anything of importance. He made an educated guess that they contained information on Papi's role in the military but to what extent? Daniel didn't know for sure, but the way his parents had reacted insinuated that there was something important and something worth concealing. *Was he a stolen baby?* He didn't think so, only because if that were the case Mama would have thrown the boxes away years ago.

The general order of the containers was from oldest to newest on the bottom. The 1983 box was likely to be on the floor. He moved them and started a new pile until he found the right one. He used a horse brush to sweep off the accumulated dust so thick it seemed no one had touched them in ten years. When the box was clean enough, he picked it up, surprised at how light it was, and carried it to the house.

The back door was unlocked. He walked into the kitchen. There was a small plate on the counter and a yerba mate cup. He couldn't ask Mama as soon as she came into the house. Better to let her get settled first. He headed into the family room. The family room was wainscoted and painted a nice even cream color. There was a built-in bookshelf in a reading nook, her favorite place to read in the house, and a desk with her laptop and a printer on it. This seemed a good place where she could get comfortable first before he asked.

He laid a blanket down and then set the box in the middle of the room where she would see it. He sat on a loveseat, waiting only a few minutes before the back door opened and closed. Her footsteps on the tile were quiet. She always liked to change her boots in the barn, and the kitchen didn't have a proper mud room. The espresso machine whirred. He heard the fridge open and close.

"Mama, it's me, Daniel. I'm here. I've come for a visit," he called from the family room.

The kitchen became dead quiet. He imagined she had turned and was staring in his direction. She was probably holding the custom-made espresso cups that she had ordered from Argentina. Likely, she was holding one hand on her chest to control her breathing. Hopefully he hadn't scared her.

"Where are you, *mijo*?"

"I'm in the family room, Mama. Come, please."

Her heard her pad down the hallway. When she got to the family room, she started across to welcome him. She stopped when she noticed the box.

"What is this?"

"Mama, before you say no, please listen to me. I respect your wishes, but I cannot put this away. It is on my mind constantly."

"This is your last chance. If I say no, you must agree to never speak of it again."

"I agree. I have three parts I need to speak of. Will you hear all of it?"

She placed her drink on a small coffee table before settling into an overstuffed chair across from him. Her hair was pulled back neatly in a bun that would fit inside a dressage helmet. She wore light tan jodhpurs and a black shirt tucked in. Her hands were clean and her nails manicured.

"I love you, Mama. You are the woman who raised me, who bandaged my scrapes, who always cried for me on the first day of school. You are the woman whom I love in my heart, and you will always be my mama no matter what happens."

She didn't move an inch. Her back was ramrod straight, and the only indication that he had said something to sway her was a slight tremor in her breath.

"You are everything to me," he continued. "The love I have for Granpapi and Papi is what I remember as a child. When I learned Granpapi was a Nazi, I couldn't believe it, even when I saw the pictures. This man slept next to me under the stars. I idolized him. But I know this now. I understand the truth. I still love him, but it's different."

Mama got up and walked to the bookshelf. There was a picture of Daniel and his granpapi in a hug in front of Daniel's favorite horse Habi, short for Habenero. There was another of Papi lifting Daniel into the air. She took down a picture of her and Papi on horses at the *estancia*. "I had no idea, either, not until many years later with all the news reports about Nazi's coming into Argentina, the sympathizers and officers looking to escape their fate. But once I knew ..." She looked away and steeled her jaw.

Daniel stood next to her and held out another picture frame. It was a black-and-white photo of the whole family before Thomas and Camila had died. It was so long ago, and yet he could vividly recall Thomas racing with him to school and Camila's love for animals. She was always bringing home injured birds and had earned the nickname *Curandera* or Healer.

"The curse, Mama. This is a way to end it."

"The curse isn't real. Our lives are fine. Stop kicking dead dogs and let them lie."

"Let us find out the truth. Let us help others to find closure."

"Will you do the genetic test?"

He nodded. "Mama, this box is between us. It is only a box, but the seed is planted. The doubt I have inside me is a terrible thing and will fester. I want to root it out, but I cannot without definitive truth."

"Are these scars on my belly not enough for you?"

"Please, I don't do this to tarnish you. You are my mama. You will always be, no matter what the test says. But I have to be certain."

"You are not certain of my love for you?"

"That is not it. Trust me. We must do this. I will

speak to Paloma. She is with the Grandmothers of the Plaza. We will find something acceptable."

Mama stood and walked to the box. She circled it and then kneeled in front of it. Daniel started toward her, but she held up her hand.

"No, this is my job to protect you. How can I protect you if I let this box go? I couldn't control his temper. I knew so much but said nothing."

He didn't answer. Keeping silent was one way to contain the past. But he did not want that life--that polite way of walking around each other, manners the only bond between him and his mama. The Grandmothers had assured him so much good would come. The truth would set so many free. Parents could find closure. Releasing the past took away its power.

Mama hit the box once and then twice, until she was beating it with both hands, her hair wild as her fists flew in the air. "I hated you! I knew you, bastard. *Anda a la concha de tu madre.* They say you get what you deserve in this life, but how easy for you. To have a life you do not remember."

Daniel let her get all of it out--the tears as they streamed down her face, the anger in her hands and heart. She stood and gave the box a final kick for good measure. And when she was finished, he held out his arms. She turned and hugged him, so tightly he couldn't breathe. He thought she'd never let go.

"*Mijo*, I need time. I love you, but you have to go." She disentangled herself from his arms and put her palms flat on his chest, tapping him gently.

"And Daniel, let me remind you. This life is short. Do what you must. I will do the same."

*E*leanor spent Sunday buying groceries and paying bills. In the afternoon, she took a walk around the neighborhood. Her date with Daniel had been amazing and wonderful, and all she could think about was repeating it on an infinite loop if possible. What she liked most about him was his sense of humor, the way he made her smile, and she didn't find much funny. She remembered waking up with him, his sweet expression, the way his olive skin looked exotic to her. Her thoughts weren't heavy with the burden of marriage like they were on most of her dates sanctioned by her mother.

Like the one with Abraham. It was set for Monday night, but Eleanor was still working out the logistics with him. If she won BINGO, she'd have an "in" with Jack Donohoe. Maybe her mother would actually be proud of her. Maybe her mother would stop trying to set her up.

She had slept well, considering, and went into work early. Even though her major deliverables were completed, the added stress of winning BINGO while trying to sell her app was distracting her from answering emails, and she wanted to catch up. There was a morning meeting with Katherine and the staffers for an update on the Vegas trip. She gathered her things and made her way to the meeting room.

The first to arrive for the meeting, she set up her laptop. The room was dark mahogany with a series of Revolutionary War paintings on one wall. The other wall had no art due to a large retractable screen for a projector. Opal and Kat came in together. They were in deep conversation, but Kat managed to wave hello. Madeline, Chloe and Cheyenne were the last to arrive. Liz was nowhere to be found. The Chinese gig was supposed to be over, but maybe she was taking a personal day after working all weekend. Chloe was cheery and bouncy, saying hi to everyone as she entered. She set her things next to Eleanor. Cheyenne sat next to her. Eleanor got a text notification on her cell and saw that it was Daniel.

Daniel: *Morning galgita. I have something special for tonight if you are free?*

She shivered as she thought of his hands on her skin. The memory of Daniel's hands on her body was so vivid it almost felt as if he were tracing a finger over her now. Eleanor couldn't help but smile. She couldn't believe her fate in finding Daniel even if he was the wrong man for her—at least according to her mother.

Eleanor: *Yes. I'm free.*

She couldn't wait to see him.

Daniel: *The taste of you is still in my mouth.*

Her lips opened slightly, but then she remembered where she was. Everyone in the office was staring at her. She placed the phone back on the table, screen down. This meeting was important. Now was not the time. She needed to be present even if her body wasn't.

"Are you going to join us?" asked Katherine, who stood at the head of the table.

"Of course. A moment, please." Eleanor pulled out her research notes regarding SUNFLOWER. "Here are the full bios you requested. I've connected with the hotels in Las Vegas to make sure technical setups are taken care of. We'll have password-required Wi-Fi, staff elevator passcodes, and other IT protocols. Also,

I'm looking into other security concerns that could arise."

"Thank you," Katherine said. "Can you put your research up on the screen?"

"Sure, hold on." Eleanor took the cord from the projector and placed it into her computer. After clicking a few buttons, her laptop was displayed for all to see. Her phone dinged a notification and she checked it quickly. It was Abraham.

"Eleanor? The research."

"Sorry," she said. "I was just putting it on vibrate." She placed her phone in her pocket.

"Chloe, get a copy from Eleanor. Make sure you and Harrison review it as well."

Chloe responded with a brief nod. Harrison, the environmental lawyer assigned to the case, had helped Chloe to avoid some of the lobbyists around Capitol Hill. The bios were primarily for her, but Katherine wanted everyone to review them for good measure.

Madeline held up her hand. "I'd like to look at it as well to make sure it meshes with the PR message we're preparing to send out."

"Of course. I'll email it to you," Eleanor said.

"Since the BINGO game is nearly finished, we are still going to use it as the determining factor for who goes to Vegas," Katherine said. She looked at Eleanor first. "How many letters do you have?"

"I have four," Eleanor said with a tiny smile. "And I've got my last one scheduled for . . ." Her smile faded with the realization that she had a date with both Abraham and Daniel that evening. She *had* to go out with Abraham if she wanted to set the relationship with her mother right. And if she wanted to win BINGO. She had to cancel her plans with Daniel.

"It's going to be close then, isn't it?" Madeline said. "I have a date tomorrow night after my PR meeting. We might be racing for the win Tuesday, Eleanor."

"Not so fast," said Cheyenne. "I'm right on all your tails."

"Very well," Katherine said. "If this game is over sooner rather than later, all the better. I am looking forward to seeing who'll win."

"It sure has been an interesting contest," Cheyenne said. "Do you think it'll go to the wire?"

"It's still fair game. No one has it in the bag yet." The women started side-talking, trying to figure out who had the best chance of winning.

Katherine clapped her hands to get everyone's attention. "Let's get back to work, shall we? Anyone else with updates?" No one spoke. "That's a wrap then, ladies. See you later."

As people were getting up to leave, Eleanor's phone vibrated, causing everyone to watch her. Kat gave her a dirty look, and this time Madeline joined her. Eleanor mouthed "work" and checked the message. Suddenly, her mood changed. Abraham had texted again.

The women filed out of the room and within a few minutes, Eleanor was alone. She wanted to finish texting before heading back. She hit the reply button. She'd have to accept the date for tonight, she had said yes to him first, and felt compelled to honor that. And she wanted to win the game.

> ***Eleanor***: *I'm free tonight at 6:30.*
> ***Abraham***: *Sure. Do you have a favorite restaurant?*

"Dammit!" she said aloud, not wanting to meet up with him. Didn't her mother, Mrs. Rebekah Winslow, have anything else to do in life besides bake bialys and pester her to marry a good Jewish boy? Her mother needed a new hobby to replace the goal of marrying her off. Perhaps if she bought her mother a camera, her mom would take it up as a new hobby, but it was more likely she would only use it to take pictures of suitable Jewish men. Maybe Eleanor could connect her with Cheyenne on the baking stuff. Cheyenne had mentioned a Smithsonian event coming up focused on the history of baking. Her mother and Mrs. Stein could go.

Eleanor had gathered her things and started back to the office when Daniel called. At the sight of his name, her body responded, wanting his touch. She tried to shake it off before picking up.

"*Dulce galgita.* I have missed your voice."

"I can't," she said, stopping suddenly in the hallway. Annoyed grunts sounded as people sidestepped her. "My mother has set me up on a date. Apparently, she traded her special bialy recipe for a date for me with Mrs. Stein's cousin's son."

"Only one recipe?" he said. "I would barter a whole cookbook if that is the going price."

"Very funny. Anyway, the date is tonight so I can win BINGO." She pinched the phone between her head and shoulder, then smoothed the sides of her pants.

"Well, it is only to kiss, right? This is nothing. But the surprise can only happen tonight. Can you reschedule your date for tomorrow?"

"If I'm going to win BINGO, I have to go out tonight. Madeline has a date lined up for tomorrow night for her last kiss. I have to beat her. I could win."

"Then schedule an afternoon coffee with him. Where is the kiss supposed to happen?"

"The Franklin Delano Roosevelt Memorial. Hold on, I remember something." Eleanor switched menus and Googled "DC PR Association meeting." Madeline had mentioned she would go there first. The website popped up, and she navigated to the calendar page. The meeting started at 6:30 p.m. As long as she got her kiss before seven, she would win. And she could go out with Daniel.

"I don't know. It's close," she said.

"Come with me. It will be fine. Make the date earlier. You'll win. I want to see you."

"You really don't care if I kiss him?" she asked, unsure of how she felt. On one hand, she loved the way he made her feel, the way he touched her, but she had promised herself that Daniel was not a long-term affair. It was another thing if he didn't want her.

"You will not take him home with you, no?"

"Who? Abraham? No, that won't happen. But you don't care?"

"A little kiss is of no importance," he said. "If you must go on a date to win BINGO and also to appease your mother, I am not concerned."

Eleanor twirled a pen between her fingers.

"Do not worry about this. My mother is the same. She would barter me for a Santiago cake recipe. You will see. Abraham is only a date. We will have our own fun tonight, yes?" His voice dropped an octave. "There are many things to be concerned with, but a date with a good Jewish boy? Nothing to worry about."

"Okay, but this better be worth it."

Eleanor finished her normal workload and her to-do list before sending Abraham a text. They agreed to move the date to Tuesday evening. She could still win BINGO by tomorrow night, but it made her nervous to wait when she could so easily win the game and have the opportunity to work with the Donohoes. Tomorrow she'd meet Abraham, win BINGO, and focus on other things. Like her seating-chart app. Like Daniel's hands on her body.

On her walk home, she texted Daniel and asked for the dress code. At home, in her bathroom, she fixed her hair and put on makeup. She had decided to wear jeans and found her tightest, most expensive pair. They hugged her ass perfectly and fit her waist comfortably but snugly. Then she threw on a Michael Stars T-shirt. She wasn't usually a stiletto heel kind of girl but believed it should be a staple in every girl's closet. Besides, she smiled knowingly, Daniel would appreciate them. She put on a pair of strappy Jimmy Choo heels that she'd purchased on a shopping day with Madeline. Luckily, they'd been on sale. She looked classic, old-school American.

She poured herself a glass of water and opened the refrigerator to get a lemon slice while waiting for Daniel to pick her up. A shiver ran through her body as she remembered the way he had held her, the way he touched her like no one else. That breakfast. Her mom walking in. She cringed as she squeezed the lemon into the water. Was he going to become a long-term relationship or was he a fling? Did she care about Daniel enough to go through the maelstrom of her mother's dislike that alternated between chilly silence and cutting words?

If her mother's mercurial temper were aimed solely at her, she could probably take it. She had before, and it would be difficult but not impossible. Her mother had been known to slash at others, not just her. Eleanor had no wish to put Daniel through that. Besides, she wasn't sure if he'd stick around after another bout with her mother. He had already weathered one storm, but she should break up with him and save everyone the heartache. She heard a knock and was startled from her thoughts. She answered the door.

He stepped back to take her in, letting out a whistle. "You look amazing," he said with a low growl.

She reached to take the bottle of wine he had in his hand. "I'll pour us a glass."

"Hmm, those shoes," he said, pulling her into his arms. "If my little surprise wasn't so good, I'd suggest staying in."

"You'll have to be patient, dear," she said with a teasing smile.

"Do I?" He closed the distance between them and kissed her on the neck below her ear.

"Your charms won't work on me," she lied, pretending as if his kiss didn't exhilarate her.

His lips touched her ever so lightly, sending ripples down her spine. He whispered, his breath warm. "When my charms do work, I hope you're ready."

He released her, and she felt like she'd lost something, but he was right in front of her. *Patience is a virtue.* With a deep breath, she moved to get two glasses out of the cupboard, knowing the end of the evening would be spectacular, knowing she would be naked in his arms soon enough.

While drinking wine, Eleanor tried to trick him into giving up the details for the surprise date, but he wouldn't give one iota of information. The cab driver called to let them know he was out front, and they were on their way. Daniel gave the location to the driver by showing him what was on his phone screen. They crossed the bridge into the city and stopped at the corner of U Street and 9th at a place called Nelly's.

The bar itself was a white building with a black awning over the windows. Bright neon signs were plastered in the window. It reminded Eleanor of pictures she had seen from New Orleans' French Quarter. Once inside, curved arches of gingerbread decorated the doors. The crowd was young and happily drunk. There were signs advertising a drag queen show upstairs every Monday night. The show tune music was loud, and the line was long.

"This is it."

"Could you imagine our mothers here?" Eleanor asked. "They would be so scandalized."

"Yes, they would," he said with a wry smile. "But tonight isn't them. The real surprise for you is in the back."

He led Eleanor through the crowd to where poker was being played. There was a single table set up with a dealer. Five players were at the table with various cards. She was surprised he had remembered her offhand comment about playing poker. She hadn't played in a long time. It was a nice gesture, but jeez, she could have won BINGO. Yet Daniel was so excited about bringing her here and so happy she didn't say anything.

"Did you want me to teach you how to play?" she asked.

"No, I want to watch you. I love seeing your smile."

Placing her hand on her hip she said, "You like to watch, do you?" Her words felt fake. She was trying to be happy, but she wanted the BINGO game to be over and that could've happened if she had gone out with Abraham. *Okay, so instead I'm here with Daniel.* She wanted to be more appreciative but couldn't help but feel annoyed.

The Texas Hold'em poker game was between deals, and a young man left an open seat. Daniel directed her into the chair and put down a hundred-dollar bill on the table.

"Let's see what you got."

The dealer took the money and changed it into poker chips for her. The dealer dealt out two cards face down to the players. After the first-round betting, the dealer laid the three cards up in front of him called the flop cards. Another round of betting ensued, and then the dealer laid down the fourth card.

Eleanor now had three of a kind, which was pretty damn good but not great.

One girl giggled uncontrollably. With an annoyed sigh, Eleanor fingered the corner of each card. This game had better be worth losing BINGO over. She couldn't decide if the giggling girl was playing her for a fool or was smart enough to appreciate a good hand, or if she was silly and drunk and just playing at the behest of her friends who goaded her by chanting her name. Eleanor blocked her out and honed in on the cards. A player called, and they showed their hands. Little Miss Drunkie also had three of a kind--and a higher match than Eleanor's. She had lost.

"So close. That was great card playing!" Daniel said, patting her back.

She narrowed her eyes at him. Was that a guy pat? She let out a sigh of frustration. Poker was usually fun, but tonight she was having a hard time feeling the excitement. And she didn't need Daniel to be conde-scending.

"I'm going to get us a drink. Play another round?" he asked.

"No, thanks. Let's go."

They walked toward the bar, and Daniel lightly muscled his way through the shoulder-to-shoulder crowd. Then he stopped. A gorgeous woman stood in front of him. She had long brown hair that curled perfectly near her waist. She was the kind of woman pirates would risk mutiny for. Eleanor could have sworn her eyes were iridescent, a light green that reminded Eleanor of a cat and then, if that weren't enough, she had perfect, plush lips. Her shirt was unbuttoned to show off her cleavage. A crucifix dangled from her neck.

The woman kissed him. On the lips. He didn't even try to swerve away. It was only a peck, but for damn sure that kiss was more than friendly. Daniel patted Valentina's back, too, and it was a sweet, loving pat rather than the friendly thump he had given Eleanor earlier.

"Ah, Eleanor, this is my good friend Valentina. We knew each other in Buenos Aires."

"That's nice," Eleanor replied, a little more tersely than she intended. *Something* had to be wrong with Valentina. Maybe she was crazy. Maybe she was stupid. She was so perfect. Eleanor wasn't sure why Daniel would ever choose her over this gorgeous creature.

"Hello. So glad to meet you," Valentina said. "Danny and I met when we were nine. We took confirmation together."

Eleanor tried to find a smirk on Valentina's face, but she looked . . . friendly. Eleanor briefly smiled back.

"The nuns. Do you remember? They were awful," Daniel said.

"You were awful. I don't think a day went by you didn't get in trouble!" Valentina laughed and rested her hand on his forearm.

"But luckily my charm worked well."

"Not on Sister Maria. I don't think even think God's charm would have worked on her." Valentina threw her hair back and gave a velvety laugh. The action was intoxicating. How could any man resist her? Eleanor wished she could grow her hair out long so she could do that, too.

"We used to date," Daniel said, "but that was a long time ago."

Eleanor watched him carefully. He was obviously happy to see Valentina, but Eleanor wasn't sure if he was happy to see Valentina as a friend, or if he thought they should rekindle their old relationship.

"I ended up working for United Airlines' head-quarters here in DC on the marketing team, and I learned from friends that Danny works at the embassy. I've been hoping to run into him for ages now." Valentina's flawless, perfectly painted vermillion lips smiled at Eleanor.

Danny? What was up with that? Eleanor wished for a gash of lipstick on the other woman's perfectly white teeth, but of course there wasn't one.

"Roberto is coming," Valentina said. "He is recently divorced. Did you know this? Oh, look! He's over there."

Behind Valentina, Eleanor saw a tall Latino with his hands raised in the air. He was just as gorgeous as

Valentina. *Was he out of a freaking soap opera? Was this some weird Telenova episode?* He came over and gave Daniel a warm hug and then kissed Valentina's lips.

After a quick introduction to Eleanor, the conversation continued between the three Argentinians about their old friends back home. While Eleanor knew Latinos tended to be touchy-feely, she did not like having Valentina's hands on Daniel one bit. The crowded bar pushed the three friends together while separating Eleanor from the group. She didn't like feeling left out and was about to excuse herself when Daniel reached through the separation and brought her back.

"My friend Roberto test-drives cars for BMW in Argentina. He's a professional race car driver. He let me borrow one of his cars this afternoon."

"I can hot wire cars," Eleanor said.

The conversation came to a stop. Valentina, Daniel and Roberto looked at her.

"I have to go to the bathroom," she said, awkwardly looking around. "I don't see it."

"It's in that corner." Daniel turned her shoulders to aim her in the right direction.

He seemed a little quick to help her out. Was he trying to get rid of her? She should have stuck to her guns and gone out with Abe tonight. She'd be giving him a kiss about now and winning BINGO. She dodged and weaved between people, the odd bump or two aggravating her as she went through the crowd.

Once in the stall, she checked her watch. It was 9:30 already, too late to text Abraham for a change in plans. Her mother was right—she should stick to what she knew. She should only date nice Jewish boys because then at least expectations would be met.

She put her face in her hands. A possible future with Daniel was nothing but heartache. With a loud sigh, she put on some lip gloss, and calm came over her. This was silly. She was overreacting. Out of the stall, she adjusted her expression in the mirror to its usual stoic calm. *Everything will be fine.*

On her way back, she saw Valentina was still there, still being her overfriendly, touchy self. Daniel held her hand for fuck's sake. Maybe he was patting it like Valentina was an old lady, but still, he certainly seemed to be enjoying her attention, as did Roberto. This three-ring circus had no room for one more. That was it, Eleanor thought. She'd had enough. She was leaving.

But by the time she got to Daniel, ready to say goodnight, his friends were excusing themselves.

"It was so nice to meet you," Valentina gushed at Eleanor. "Roberto and I have to go. I do hope we get to see you again." She leaned in and gave Eleanor a kiss on each cheek.

"Thank you," Eleanor said, reluctantly turning her head for the cheek kiss.

"Danny," said Valentina as she offered her cheek to him to be kissed in turn, "you and Eleanor should come with us."

"Yeah, man. You should come," Roberto said. "The test races in Delaware are over, and drivers from all over the country are in town. You'd love meeting them. We're gathering in Adams Morgan."

"Sure, let's go. Eleanor, you ready?"

She had grown up around cars, and the idea of being with a bunch of professional race car drivers sounded fun, but she was tired, and she was pissed. The night was supposed to be Daniel's special surprise for her, and the whole night seemed to be a comedy of errors. The hand of poker had been mildly fun, but she had lost. After watching Daniel and Valentina together, surely he wasn't interested in Eleanor beyond just a good time. He was everything her mother had warned her about.

"You go ahead. I need to go home. Early meetings."

"Let's both go with them. It'll be fun."

And spend the rest of the evening being a third wheel? No thank you. "I'm tired. I want to go home."

Daniel stood back with his brows furrowed. "What are you talking about?"

"Danny, um, we're going to leave," Valentina said. She directed her words to Eleanor. "It was nice to meet you."

"Eleanor, nice to meet you, too. See you guys soon," said Roberto. Valentina linked her arm through his. They gave each other a glance, *that kind of glance,* and then Valentina turned to look at Daniel questioningly.

"You don't have to stay for me," Eleanor said to him. "It seems to me you'd rather--"

Daniel waved goodbye. Valentina smiled kindly, and she and Roberto turned tail to leave.

"Spit it out, Eleanor. You are the most direct person I know. This isn't like you at all."

"Nothing is wrong. You want to go with them. I don't."

"She is my old girlfriend. There is nothing between us. Roberto and I are friends. That is all."

Eleanor didn't feel like a grown woman at that moment. She felt small and inconsequential like she had when kids on the playground used to call her Ellie the Porky Jew. And she hadn't even been fat, which had made her even angrier at the childish taunts.

"I have to go home," she said, looking for the exit. "I don't feel well."

She didn't belong with him. Her mother was right. They had nothing in common. They had dissimilar interests. She hadn't felt included and, even if it was stupid, she felt ugly next to Valentina. She turned and walked through the crowd. People parted to let her slip through. Even though she was in a crowd, she felt alone. She heard him calling her name but didn't stop. She escaped the bar and jumped into a waiting cab, not wanting him to catch up. On the ride back to her house, her stomach was upset, like a hard rock inside. He'd never call again. But at least she'd left him. Besides, she had a date with a nice Jewish boy tomorrow night. What had happened tonight was all for the better.

Eleanor turned off her phone. By the time she got home, she had a terrible headache. She sat on the edge of her bed and rubbed her temples with the heels of her hands. Her room still smelled of Daniel. The bathrobe hung on a nearby hook. She opened a window to let fresh air in. She tossed the bathrobe into the hallway and shut the door.

After she got into bed, sleep eluded her for most of the night. She worried about her mother and how to repair their relationship. She worried that she had lost her BINGO chance. She didn't like the way she had handled things with Daniel. When she finally did get to sleep, she didn't hear the alarm clock in the morning. She was exhausted, late for work, and the rest of her morning didn't get any better. The Metro was crowded. Everything took three times longer than normal. By the time she turned her phone back on, she had three missed texts from Daniel.

Daniel: Where are you?

Daniel: Please call me.

Daniel: Are you okay?

She sat in an orange Metro seat and stared at her device. She didn't respond. She wanted to but wasn't sure what to say. In the light of day, her jealousy over Valentina was petty and embarrassing. Why had she been so afraid to talk to Daniel last night? It would have been so much easier to have a conversation, but her body had been so flooded with adrenaline that talking wasn't an option. It wasn't like she planned to have such intense emotions for him.

Eleanor had thought it would be an easy love affair. She could have a fling and then get back to dating a good boy approved by her mother. She had just met Daniel. How could she have such strong feelings for a man she had met only a week ago? Besides, he shouldn't be standing in the way of what she wanted, career-wise, anyway.

For her, BINGO provoked her competitive streak. And she had wanted to meet Donohoe, the automotive industry leader, because she had a childhood fascination for him. The Donohoe name reminded her of time spent with her dad when they worked on cars together. She wanted to impress her mother too. She knew getting a job with the Donohoes would do that, and after this last encounter between her mother and Daniel, she wanted to show her mother that she could go above and beyond. A job like that would be the icing on the cake.

In retrospect, she would have loved to go with Daniel and meet Roberto's friends, but the evening hadn't turned out. By the time she'd gotten home, the events had clarified what she had to do. She had to break up with Daniel. She had no real reason to break up with him, had only weak excuses, and she knew it, but she was embarrassed to own up. Did she really care about BINGO? Did she really want to go to Vegas? Did she really care about meeting the Donohoes, or was that some flimsy excuse, too? What was her end game? She wasn't sure. And the last thing she needed was a bunch of silly emotions overriding her logic. Either way, Daniel had to go.

She arrived at the Cannon Building and checked her phone to see where exactly her work meeting was to take place. After reading her online schedule, she headed straight for the conference room. The door was open, which meant she was not late. Chloe was already inside. Eleanor found a seat at the table and got out her laptop. As she waited for the others, she studied a Revolutionary War painting depicting Washington crossing a stormy river. She felt an odd bond with it, as if somehow she knew what it was like to be unsure of where the boat would land exactly but realizing she had to cross.

Cheyenne came into the room and set up across from her. Eleanor's phone buzzed.

Cheyenne caught her eye. "Daniel?" she mouthed.

Eleanor shrugged as if she didn't care and checked her messages.

Daniel: Please call. I don't know what happened.

Eleanor swallowed and then with a sigh switched her settings to vibrate. The idea of breaking up with him was unwanted but necessary. The problem was that she didn't have an exact reason to break up with him. "My mother doesn't like you," made her sound like a juvenile. "You are Catholic," made her sound bigoted. "Because you'll break my heart," made her sound paranoid. She'd have to think of something that sounded reasonable. But she had nothing. He was a good man and didn't deserve to be treated like this. She'd call him after the meeting and explain that the relationship was over.

"Eleanor, nice to see you. Cheyenne," Katherine said. "We're going to start without Madeline. She sent me a text saying she'd be late."

Opal and Congressman Lincoln Pierce came into the room. His charismatic personality filled the whole room. He was average height and weight. He had a strong jawline and a determined expression. There was a fierce sense of justice about him, as if he would defend a person at any cost. Media outlets had nick-named him the *Babe on the Hill* and the *Hunky Congressman*--nicknames that he himself professed to hate.

"Ladies! I must say it is good to see you all in the same room together. Kat, do we have the name of the individual who will be traveling with me to Vegas?"

"Not yet, sir," she said, her eyes steady on him. "I have an updated overview for you of the talking points for the meeting. Opal will have the logistics." She handed him a printout.

The congressman briefly glanced over the paper-work. "This looks great, Kat. Let's get to it. Read the overview aloud, please."

Kat tapped on her computer screen and pulled up the document. "Chloe Cassel and I are working on bills to create revenue and tax incentives and new jobs. With regard to the renewables legislation, we have a topnotch lawyer, Harrison Rousseau, whom we have partnered with Chloe. The two of them are making good headway." Eleanor noticed Chloe, the new intern, had a bit of a dreamy smile in response to this, and Kat cleared her throat.

"We've been able to keep the lobbyists out of this one, right? No one's the wiser?" Pierce asked.

"That's correct, sir. We had a close call with Gordy Carpenter, one of the oil and gas lobbyists, but it was resolved quickly. Eleanor has worked up profiles on Ellis and Levin Associates, so everyone knows what we are dealing with."

"Good and good. Sometimes these bills must be done in secrecy to keep the special interest money out and write a decent law that's fair to everyone. It's tough. Good work."

"Thank you," Kat said.

The door opened, and Madeline rushed in.

Opal gave her a small smile. "Madeline, we're discussing SUNFLOWER. What's the latest PR angle?"

Madeline placed her bag on the floor and got out her laptop. "No PR just yet. There are legal and tax ramifications on the table first, right Chloe? That information will impact the press release."

"Right," Chloe said, her dreamy smile replaced with a serious expression. "We'll get those to you as soon as we can."

Kat folded her hands on the table. "Harrison is reviewing our proposed legislation to ensure we don't restrict other energy resources. The principals of the bill may want us to press harder, but if we go too far, we'll be in for a bigger fight from oil and gas, and we really want to get this bill in and passed."

Pierce nodded again. "That makes sense. We've got more than one dodger at this party."

A few of the women laughed. Others nodded their heads in agreement.

Kat cleared her throat loudly. "Once we finish, I'll send the summary to Opal. Next, Eleanor is covering IT angles, security, and research. Any questions for her?"

Pierce met Eleanor's eyes and nodded. "Anything we should be aware of about Vegas, Eleanor?"

"Due to the close call that Chloe had with the lobbyists, I've compiled profiles and pulled together a portfolio of all the people attending SUNFLOWER that includes net worth, a social media profile, and specific industry-changing inventions. I've emailed the soft copy to Opal and will be sure to give you a hard copy, sir."

"Nicely done, Eleanor, thank you."

"Next, we have the marketing side of things," continued Kat. "Madeline and Cheyenne are prepping the charity lunch with appropriate press releases and other marketing angles. We might as well count Liz out. I'm dealing with the fallout--"

"Stay steady on that track, Kat," cut in the congressman. He turned to Opal. "Liz isn't available at the moment. You're fluent in Mandarin, yes?"

Opal hesitated before answering. "I majored in

Chinese in college, but I haven't used it in a few years. Thought I'd always go East, but I didn't think it'd be DC."

"You'll be perfect. You always are, Opal. You'll take over the Chinese segment from here on out. Liz will be available later this week for a debrief."

Madeline tapped the screen to put up the latest graphic. "August, the battery developer, will be building a factory in the U.S. and one in China. We have the tech colleges geared up to start ramping up the battery training along with on-the-job work programs due to the newness of the technology. Opal can manage the relationship and help get it started."

"That sounds perfect, and we'll be able to bring Yukika in as well," Opal said. "She's got the Japanese contacts we need. Madeline, send me what you have."

Pierce straightened his back and directed his next question to Kat. "Now then, ladies. I look forward to seeing who will accompany me to Vegas. We'll have an answer soon?"

"Yes, sir. The decision will be made on Friday. We will let you know. We are still . . . deciding."

"I've got all the data regarding the Service Dogs of America luncheon," started Opal, turning to Madeline. "And do you have--"

The congressional bells that signaled a vote rang through the halls.

"We'll get back to that one, Opal." The congressman gathered up his papers to place in his briefcase. "Time to go."

"Yes, sir," Opal said, before redirecting her attention to the group. "Be sure to email your summaries so I can collate them for the congressman."

"Oh, before I go," said Pierce, standing to his full height and facing Kat. "How are you all deciding who's going with me to Vegas? It's taking a long time."

Everyone in the room froze, even Kat.

"Come on, Congressman, we are going to be late if we don't leave right now," Opal said, urging him toward the door.

Pierce broke eye contact with Kat, and his gaze traveled across the table to each of the women.

"Go, sir, before the vote takes place. I'll catch up with you soon," Opal said.

Pierce's eyes landed on Opal. "I expect an answer. Let me know as soon as you can." When he left, every woman let out a collective sigh of relief.

"Meeting's over. Back to work," said Kat. "We'll know who goes to Vegas in a week."

The women quietly gathered their things and were gone. Eleanor checked her text messages. Abraham had texted her to confirm the date and time for their date that evening. She let out a sigh of resignation. She always had to do what was good for her. And so she would see Abraham to appease her mother by dating a Jewish boy. She would win BINGO and she would go on with her life.

Eleanor was alone in the room with thoughts of her life passing by. She wondered if she would regret not giving Daniel a chance. Her shoulders slumped, and she swallowed hard. She wanted to hear his laugh again. What was the worst that could happen? She picked up her smartphone and dialed Daniel's number. It went to voice mail, and she left a message.

Not a text or a call from Daniel all day. After work, Eleanor got home and flopped onto her bed. Her actions were so mercurial, not at all like her logical self. Yesterday, she didn't want anything to do with him, and now she was pining for him. Her body ached; she needed his touch. With a resigned sigh, she took a shower and then changed into a maxi skirt along with a pullover shirt for her date with Abraham. The outfit was conservative enough for a date with someone her mom had set her up with, but it also looked great.

Eleanor took the Metro downtown, and she met Abraham at a seafood restaurant near the Ronald Reagan Building. Abe was a little taller than her. He had stick-straight light brown hair, a decidedly European Roman nose and a strong jaw to boot. No beard. No sidelocks. He looked like any other modern DC male.

"I'm Abe," he said, friendly smile lines radiating from his eyes. His lips formed into a perfect bow, like Daniel's. "Only my grandmother calls me Abraham."

Like Abraham Lincoln. It dawned on Eleanor that he had the same name as the monument where she had kissed Daniel--the kiss that led to a night of dancing. The memory made her look away, but she shook it off. *What had she been thinking, getting involved with him?*

The hostess led them to a table, and they followed, somewhat awkwardly. Abe seemed sweet, though, with his kind smile. They were here at the behest of their mothers, not because they had mutual attraction. He was good-looking, but Eleanor wasn't sure she could be attracted to him. She wasn't sure what it was exactly, he hadn't done anything wrong. He was nice. He wasn't overweight or too muscular. He just ... he wasn't Daniel. She didn't want to kiss him for any reason other than to win the BINGO game.

Abe glanced at the menu and ordered a bottle of white wine and an appetizer with her nod of approval. She wasn't very hungry, at least not yet. They started learning about one other with basic questions about where they grew up, what they did for work, and what they did for fun. Like her, Abraham had emigrated from Poland to the U.S., but when he was even younger at seven. He was from a small town near hers, and he knew of her primary school. Now she understood why her mom had picked him. *Common ground.* She was sure if they dug deep enough, they'd find someone they both knew.

In an odd way, she could see herself being married to someone like him. She appraised him the way her mother might: He had a nice enthusiasm. They had similar childhood memories. He had a great body, nice teeth and was sweet. But what was he like in bed? Perfunctory?

She hadn't considered sex as part of the package until she knew how amazing it could be. A faint ache rolled over her body. Daniel was good--the way he touched her like he was meant for her. She also remembered the deep way they had connected when he shared about his mom.

"Just so you know, I'm the only tech person in our office, and I'm on call. So if my phone buzzes, I have to answer it. I'm not trying to be rude."

"Fair enough," he replied, putting a napkin in his lap.

Before she put her phone away, she saw a message flash across her screen.

Daniel: Are you there? I tried calling. Is your phone--

To get the rest of the message, she would have to unlock her phone. An image of Valentina popped into her mind. Instead of doing that, she put it down. It was ridiculous. Valentina was clearly with Roberto, but Eleanor hated the way Daniel smiled at her and the easy way he was with her. Would he be like that with all women? If she was going to have Daniel in her life, could she handle her jealousy? Why was she trying to get back with Daniel? She should get over him, starting with the handsome guy right in front of her. She was aware of her own flakiness, but at this point she couldn't entirely make up her mind if she should go with Daniel or if she should try to start over with Abe.

She scanned the menu, wanting grilled salmon, but she had to make sure there wasn't something better on the menu. Abe closed his menu. He waited patiently while she took her time.

"Where are you?" he said. "You seem a million miles away."

"It's nothing. I am trying to decide between the halibut and the salmon. It's from Scotland."

"Both sound delicious. I can't help you there."

The waiter took their order. Abe chose the vegetarian risotto, and Eleanor decided on salmon. She was quiet, and Abe steered the conversation to one of light politics and sports and then to the latest blockbuster movie. She was glad to pass the time with someone who could converse. Small talk wasn't her strong suit.

"Do you ever miss the skiing?" he asked.

Eleanor smiled. "I did. Dan--I mean a friend--told me I should get out to Colorado for real slopes."

"You haven't been yet? Eleanor, you gotta go. The Rocky Mountains are incredible. I like Montana and British Columbia. The snow is so light, like heaven."

Daniel had talked to her about skiing. Thoughts of him kept flooding her mind, but she didn't want to be rude to Abe. Nor did she want to give up her chance of a kiss and winning BINGO.

Abraham seemed excited. "It's so hard to find someone out here who appreciates skiing. I was pretty lucky. My parents took us on vacations to Utah and Colorado. As I got older, I ventured further west and discovered Red Lodge, a great little town in Montana with some sweet slopes. Then there's Whistler in B.C. Completely different vibe with upscale shopping and restaurants."

"I tried to ski in Pennsylvania," Eleanor said, "but it was all slush and ice. It was terrible. I would not waste five dollars on that."

"West Virginia isn't too far from here. Vermont's pretty good." He cast a tentative glance at her. "In a pinch, anyway. It's better than nothing."

She winced. He was so sweet. He kept reminding

her of Daniel with his lips and talk of skiing. What she needed wasn't romance. What she needed was a BINGO kiss.

"Let's go for a walk after dinner, shall we? The night is warm, and I'd really like to see the FDR Memorial. It's right off the Tidal Basin. It'll be pretty."

"Oh? That's weirdly--"

"Odd? Strange?" she said, filling in the words for him.

"Specific. Why that one?"

"I've always wanted to see it, and this would be the perfect way. No crowds, and it's not hot outside."

He shrugged with a bemused smile on his face. "Sure, can we go for a drink afterward?"

When the bill came, Eleanor put her credit card inside the check folder. Abe wouldn't hear of it, though, and replaced her card with his.

"You're right," he said. "It's a perfect night for a walk. You ready to go?"

Eleanor nodded with a slight smile. The sweltering humidity, a precursor to summer, was missing, blown away by a cool breeze. They started toward Constitution and 12th, and he took her hand. It settled comfortably in his. But she missed that sense of abandon she had with Daniel. Maybe that feeling was reckless. Maybe that feeling would end up ruining her life.

Somebody like Abe was a safe choice, someone who would be good for her.

They hailed a cab to take them the rest of the way to the FDR Memorial. They passed by the Lincoln Memorial, and Eleanor tried not to look. She tried to forget that she and Daniel had shared a sweet kiss there. The sun had not yet set; the evening was early still. She looked away and at the trees passing by. Instead of feeling calm and collected, like she knew what she wanted, her emotions felt wildly out of control.

The cab dropped them off, and they walked toward the monument. They sat on a bench near the famous statue of Franklin Delano Roosevelt and his trusty little terrier.

"Did you know the cherry trees were a gift from Japan?"

"I didn't know," she said. Eleanor liked the way Abe shared his knowledge, in small subtle droplets rather than a waterfall.

She gazed up the statue, its copper a faded light green. She didn't want to think about how the kiss with Abe would transpire. Should she wait for him or just make the move? Tired of indecision, she turned his face toward her, closed her eyes and kissed him squarely on the lips. His lips felt different from Daniel's. They felt rougher and less sensuous.

"My facts are pretty good, but I didn't know they were worthy of a kiss," Abe said with a baffled expression.

"I, uh, needed to kiss you."

"For what?"

She looked into his earnest brown eyes and had to tell him. The end result would be better if she told him about Daniel rather than the BINGO game.

"I have a lover," she said, deliberately using the scandalous word. Technically, lover was truer than boyfriend, even if she was unsure she and Daniel were together. "He's gentile, and I'm not sure if I should date him. I'm sorry. I wanted to see--"

"You what?" He sat back. "You wanted to see if kissing me would make you feel any different?"

"Yes. You're everything my mother wants for me," she said, turning away. "I wanted to be honest with you."

"This isn't a great way to start a relationship. You know that, right?"

"Just don't tell my mother. Or your mother, for that matter."

"It's all right. I won't," he said. Then he laughed. "Well, I feel like an ass now. I'm here under false pretenses, too. It wouldn't have worked for us romantically."

"Wait ... what?"

"Not that you aren't beautiful, absolutely stunning if I may say so, but I'm in love with someone else."

Eleanor didn't realize it, but she had been holding her breath. She exhaled, and her shoulders relaxed.

"Wait, hold on a second." She turned to him in relief. "You're here to please your mother, too?"

Their eyes met, and they laughed. Eleanor's heart lightened. She wasn't alone in all this.

Eleanor wiped away tears. "Who is she?"

"She's a woman I met here in DC. She's getting her Ph.D. in Maryland."

"Why are you here, then?"

"It's just easier this way. I go out on a date. It's usually boring. We have dinner and then go home. Then my mom leaves me alone for a few months."

"Daniel's Catholic. My mom doesn't like him. Then she set up this date with you and silently threatened me with expulsion from the family if I didn't go."

"You're kidding? My mother is about to lose her mind. She knows Caitlin, my girlfriend. Just so you know, you're worth one family schnitzel recipe."

"Shut up," she said, giggling. "My mother traded me for a bialy recipe. Abe, I like you. If you ever need a cover, I'll go so you can appease your mom. Yes? Friends?"

"Friends."

"Good. Let me take a selfie of the monument."

"You're weird," he said.

"It's for a friend." She was about to post it but hesitated. Daniel would see the picture. She was about to turn off her phone when another partial message showed up.

Daniel: I don't want you to play the game. I want--

He didn't want her to play the game? What the actual hell? He'd adopted such a team-player attitude, not caring who she kissed, that his reversed position at such an inconvenient time pissed her off. Why couldn't he have said that in the first place?

But Madeline was going to win then. If Eleanor didn't submit a picture, it was game over for her. For the moment, she wasn't going to submit her BINGO win. He would see the picture and know she'd posted it after his text message. Could she and Daniel be something more? She wasn't prepared to ignore her mother's wishes, though. That road would be so hard, and at the end of it, what would there be? Would Daniel be able to handle the crazy that was her mother? Would she? Eleanor turned off her phone.

"Eleanor?" Abe put a hand on her forearm, bringing her back to the real world. "Are you okay? You're looking a little pale."

She put her hand on top of his and squeezed. "I'm fine. But I'm going to take a raincheck on that drink, okay?" She stood and scanned the horizon, wondering if she should take a cab or use Uber. "I'm tired."

"That'll be easier for me, too. Let's keep in touch. Call me if you ever need anything." Abe swooped in for a friendly hug, and Eleanor gave him a kiss on the cheek goodbye.

The kitchen was her first stop. Dinner had been good but small and elegant. She needed to eat something. She got out a wine glass. Part of her felt relieved that she didn't have to play anymore. She had probably lost her chance to meet the Donohoe family. Setting the glass on the countertop, she checked her phone and reread Daniel's text. The grown-up in her knew she should call him. If she really wanted a relationship with him, she'd have to talk to him.

But had she let it go too long? Would he still answer? She wanted to call him but was afraid. From the refrigerator, she pulled out her last bialy and poured the last of the Argentine wine Daniel had brought. The two didn't pair together well, but it was what she wanted. And why the hell couldn't she have both?

She knew why. Instead Of calling, she finished her bialy, drank the glass of wine and went to bed.

The alarm went off, a sharp buzzing that almost always jolted Eleanor awake. Soft sounds never worked. The sun was out, and a soft breeze wafted through an open window. She rose and shut it before the air inside her townhome turned humid.

She dressed in a pair of navy blue slacks and a printed top from H&M along with her favorite kicks from Vans. Since she was IT, there was flexibility in her dress code. On her way to work, the sky was cerulean blue. Bright, late spring flowers had already bloomed, but everything seemed so distant.

A crow flew above her. A dog barked. Cars drove by. Normal sounds seemed so far from her thoughts that she glanced quizzically at the animals. By the time she got into the office, the sounds were replaced with the busyness of the Cannon Building: people walking in a hurry and talking on their phones.

In Pierce's office, Chloe was hard at work on her computer, her expression intense. Cheyenne, well, Cheyenne never got ruffled. Her confidence always came through. Madeline looked like a bull coming down Pamplona's ancient roads. The best course of action was to step aside.

Madeline passed her and was on her way. What was she so mad about? Madeline should be happy if she had won BINGO. But as long as it didn't involve Eleanor, she was grateful. She set up her computer and while it booted up checked Instagram on her phone. Madeline hadn't won. What??

Eleanor printed out a document for an upcoming meeting and was headed to the print room when she encountered Kat. Katherine followed her in and fiddled with the top of her to-go coffee mug. "Eleanor, I'm only here for a few minutes before I head to the hearing. But I need to speak with you in private. The conference room across the hall is free. Meet me there in a minute, okay?"

"Will this take long? I have a meeting that starts at nine."

"You'll make it."

Eleanor stopped at the breakroom to grab a coffee. She walked through the office, and Chloe gave her a look like she knew what Katherine needed to talk to her about. The look reminded Eleanor of a deer stuck in the headlights--it wasn't comforting. She crossed the hall and stepped into the conference room.

There was something strange about meeting in a conference room with only two people, as if the space was not fulfilling its purpose. She sat in a plush office chair and pulled out her phone to check on work emails. On her main screen, she encountered an unanswered text message from Daniel this morning.

Daniel: *Answer me. I don't deserve this.*

It was true, and she did not want to end their relationship. But she wasn't going to post her picture with Abe, either.

Kat swung the heavy door open, and it shut behind her. She set her computer bag on the table and pulled out a chair, swiveled it toward Eleanor and sat. "Please don't look so worried. Everything is fine." Kat crossed her legs and brushed back a few loose hairs.

Eleanor held the warm ceramic cup in her hand. She took a deep breath and lowered her shoulders. "Well then, tell me."

"Direct like a New Yorker. Sometimes I think you're in the wrong town."

Eleanor knitted her brows at the response. She

ought to think about moving to a new town, a new state. That would solve the problem of her mother, at least geographically. No, that was grasping at straws. Her mother would follow her across the globe if she moved. The only place she might escape her mom was to return to Poland, and that wasn't about to happen.

"Let's get to it. Carleen, *my boss,* knows about the game. We had to tell her yesterday."

Eleanor stood and spilled some of her coffee. "Are we fired? Are you getting rid of--"

Kat uncrossed her legs and rose enough to pat her on the shoulder. "No, no. That's not it. Sit back down. Please."

"The game will play out for those of you who want to continue. But it must be discreet. If this gets out at all to the public--if Gretchen, our favorite social blogger finds out--we are all toast."

"That's all you wanted to tell me?" Eleanor asked, unable to believe there wasn't more. Carleen didn't put up with any shit. The fact that Kat was letting this game continue at all was weird. The logic didn't compute. She was surprised that the congressman hadn't sent them all a nasty email about it yet.

"Why keep playing? Wouldn't it be easier to cut the game and send the most appropriate person?"

"I suppose so, but . . . well, it's over in a few days. I'm just saying don't get caught."

"Are you no longer playing? You make it sound like you are done with this."

Kat shrugged. "My priorities have shifted. I'm taking myself out of the running for Vegas."

"Why would you do that?"

Kat sighed and stood. "I have my reasons. Just be careful, Eleanor."

Her reasons? "Okay." Eleanor was on the verge of telling Kat that she had already gotten the last BINGO kiss. Her mind raced through the actions she'd have to take. She'd have to post the picture of her and Abe on Instagram. And then Daniel would know. It would sever the last link between them. That wasn't what she wanted. Even if she wanted to win, she didn't want to disrespect him. She'd call him tonight. Even if she had no idea what the hell she wanted, she'd call him and at least talk.

"Madeline has plausible deniability. You helped her delete the soft copies. I advise that you shred your BINGO card. We want no evidence. I'm off to my hearing. Text me if you have any questions." Kat gathered her things and left before Eleanor could say goodbye.

ELEANOR HEADED BACK to the breakroom for a refill

of her coffee before distracting herself with work. The pot was empty, so she set it up for a fresh brew. Just as the machine wheezed into life, Cheyenne came in with a plate of colorful French macaroons.

"I made these last night. Would you like one?"

Eleanor selected a bright blue one and bit into it. "These are ridiculously delicious. Please tell me you are going to quit someday and open a bakery."

Cheyenne's face transformed with a huge grin. "I should, right?" She bit her lip as though she were considering saying something. "I love teaching for now, though. I've got a great beginner pie class this weekend—it's just a one-off. And then next week I start this amazing collaboration at the Smithsonian. You should totally come to my pie class, though. A lot of babes register for my class. You could come with Daniel. It'd make a really fun date."

Eleanor squirmed in her chair. The phone felt heavy in her hand, so she placed it on the desk. "I don't know about that. I'm not much of a cook--baker--what's the right word?"

"Baker will do."

"I'm not much of anything in the kitchen. My mom makes amazing baked goods—challah, bialys, strudels--that kind of thing."

"Mmm, nothing better than a good challah. We do get older guys, too. Maybe I should try to set her up?"

Eleanor almost laughed. She couldn't imagine her mother on a date at all, but maybe it was time to help her mom find a new hobby, meet new people. It would be nice for her. "Actually ... can you email me the info?"

"I'd love to get your mom in the kitchen. She might teach me a thing or two, you never know," Cheyenne said. "Oh, that's right, I almost forgot to ask. I heard from Madeline that you made this cool app you're trying to sell?"

"Her dad is interested in it. I met him and his lead developer a few days ago."

"What will you do if you sell it?"

"It's not private-plane money. It will be enough to quit, though. Maybe I'll move to California. Or I'll go to mechanic school," she said on a whim.

"Mechanic school? As in car mechanics? Why would you do that?"

"I love cars. The sleek form of the older cars especially. Like those Formula One cars, the Aston Martins. I love them. My Dad and I used to work on cars together."

"Wow, I've never heard you talk about your dad before." Cheyenne shook her head with a smile. "Ha. Seems like all of us have these secret desires. How come you haven't acted on it?"

"I don't know--life--work is busy. I don't have time."

"Time. The death knell of dreams. There's always a little bit of time, even if it's not exactly what you want."

"What do you mean?" Eleanor was perplexed. Either you pursued something or you didn't. Decisions were binary.

"Why don't you go join a fancy car club or start one on Meetup? There's always a way to indulge your dreams, even if it's for a few hours. It doesn't have to be all or nothing." Cheyenne lifted the plate of macaroons for emphasis. "I bake something every day to stay sane. It's about balance."

"You're right. It doesn't take much. A little here, a little there."

"A little ingenuity." Cheyenne looked around the office as if to make sure no one else was listening. "Can I tell you a secret?"

Eleanor did not need to keep other people's secrets. But she was intrigued by Cheyenne's sudden chattiness. "Maybe, if it is nothing dangerous."

Cheyenne pursed her lips. "You know how you just said I should open a bakery? Well, it's not exactly that, but my roommates and I want to open a restaurant together. We're all saving like crazy. We live together so we can each save more money. We've got nearly a hundred thousand saved between all of us."

"Dollars? That's impressive. You don't plan on working here forever, then?"

Cheyenne sighed. "I'm slowly realizing that this," she paused and circled her arms to indicate the office as a whole, "this is more my family's dream, not mine. I belong in a kitchen. A huge, shiny, bright commercial kitchen. I just have to figure out how to make my family understand my choice."

Eleanor had thought Cheyenne had a dream life with a perfect family. Did everyone have conflict? Abe was seeing someone his mother did not approve of. Her mother wouldn't accept Daniel. Eleanor grabbed a second cookie, filled up her coffee cup, and she and Cheyenne walked back to their desks together. Eleanor felt revitalized and ready to tackle her long list of unanswered emails.

Out of the corner of her eyes she noticed a man at the front of the office trying to balance a clipboard and a huge bouquet of flowers--maroon peonies. *Did Daniel ... Was it really him?*

Chloe accepted the flowers and signed the receipt. She brought them over and put them on the only clear spot on Eleanor's desk, right in the center. "Wow, Eleanor, these are gorgeous. Lucky lady."

Eleanor stood and opened the little envelope and read the note: "Call me. D"

Cheyenne left her desk and was now standing next to Eleanor. She chirped, "I bet I know who they're from. There is only one guy Eleanor knows who is romantic enough to send flowers."

"Who?" Chloe asked, scanning from Eleanor back to Cheyenne. "You have to tell."

"I'll do no such thing," said Eleanor, giving Cheyenne a dirty look. "You'll both have to keep guessing."

Cheyenne broke into song. "Oh, Danny Boy, the pipes the pipes are calling . . ."

"Do tell. What happened?" Chloe directed her question to Cheyenne.

"Well, last week Eleanor and I went to play softball with the embassy people, and I had a BINGO kiss lined up for her. After the game, we all ended up at the bar and guess who left early?"

"We are adults here," shot back Eleanor, glaring at Cheyenne. "It is none of your business."

"Don't worry about it," Chloe said. "What you do after the bar is up to you. Damn, this BINGO game is certainly turning out to be *very* interesting."

"I've got to get back to work if you'll excuse me." Eleanor cleared a pile of papers from the corner of her desk and moved the flowers out of her workspace.

The scent of peonies filled the space around her, the way they had in her bedroom as Daniel scattered them around her naked body. The memory of the way the flowers had floated over her skin sent ripples of desire up her back, but she made sure to keep her poker face. All she could think about was Daniel. What she wanted was to be naked in his arms. The blossoms reminded her of their first night, how he used the flower to tease her, the whisper of them against her skin. *The way he touched her.* Her body turned hot. She wanted his hands to roam over her body. *The way he felt inside her.*

She got up, grabbed her phone and left. It was that simple. She needed to talk to him right away. Chloe and Cheyenne's eyes burned into her back, but they didn't say anything. She was surprised they didn't follow, but they knew the truth about her and Daniel, even if she tried to deny it. She found an empty conference room and slipped inside.

Eleanor's fingers shook as she unlocked her phone and hovered over his contact. She breathed in and out slowly, steeling herself before calling. It went straight to voice mail. Where the hell was he?

Chapter 20

Eleanor spent the rest of her day checking her phone, even though she'd set its ring on the loudest setting. She stomped home and into her kitchen and set the peonies on the counter. Their scent had taunted her all afternoon, reminding her of Daniel's touches, his caresses. And yet, he hadn't called back. Why the hell not?

First, he sent flowers asking her to call. Then, when she broke and finally contacted him, he didn't even send a text back. What was wrong with him? Was he playing games with her? Giving her a taste of her own medicine? She felt crazy being pulled in too many directions and opened her fridge with such force the condiments shook in the door. Salad. That was what she wanted. She took out a bottle of dressing and a bag of greens.

She snapped open the bag and dumped the contents into a colander. She didn't trust any pre-wash greens and always rinsed the leaves clean. Once she got the salad into a bowl and drizzled Goddess dressing over it, she happened to glance up and noticed the old peonies, the ones he had brought her before their concert date, in a vase. Her stomach thudded with such force she lost her appetite. Had she ruined everything by not calling? Isn't that what she wanted? To say goodbye and move on with her life? She wasn't supposed to want Daniel yet she did.

"Daniel. Where the hell are you?" she yelled, asking the flowers that had no answer.

Her phone started ringing. Eleanor realized she had left it by the front door in her purse. She sprinted across the kitchen and into the living room, found her purse and started to rifle through it to stop the insistent ringing. Her hand jammed into the outside pocket and then into the purse where she found it in a side pouch she usually never used.

The caller ID displayed her mom's picture. Reluctantly, Eleanor answered. Instead of being excited, she was now annoyed.

"Are you going to be home tonight?" her mother asked, foregoing any of the usual pleasantries. "Is *he* going to be there?"

"No, mother." Eleanor held in a sigh. "Daniel's not

here. But I'm kind of busy. Can't you tell me over the phone?"

"No, it's important. You need to hear this in person."

"Fine. Come on over."

Fifteen minutes later, Eleanor's doorbell rang. Normally, her mom knocked and let herself in. She was ringing to make a point--to rub in Saturday's embarrassment.

Her mom was dressed in a more formal suit with a severe skirt and boxy jacket. "Are you sure no one is here?"

"There's no one here."

"That is refreshing news. I'm glad to hear it." Her mom came inside the apartment and into the kitchen, sniffing the air. "Did you get flowers?"

"Something like that," Eleanor said, shuffling her feet.

Her mother shot her a lightning-fast glare. "I'm so glad that character Daniel is not here. Do you know him very well?"

"My co-worker Cheyenne introduced us."

Her mother walked into the living room, her nose wrinkling as she passed the couch. Eleanor knew it was killing her, that her mother was dying to go into her bedroom and investigate the sheets, but she only pursed her lips together and straightened out a pillow.

"What is it? Out with what you need to say." Eleanor was well aware of her mother's mannerisms that revealed a difficult topic she wanted to avoid.

Her mother pulled her shoulders back and grimaced. "You should know that man, that Daniel Prado? He comes from a terrible family. His grandfather was a Nazi who hid in Argentina."

"What? That's crazy." Off-kilter, Eleanor steadied herself on the back of the couch.

"I didn't trust Prado from the moment I saw him. When he said his full name, I took that as an opportunity to find out more."

"What do you mean find out more? Did you hire a private investigator?" *This was unbelievable. Did her mother have no shame? No limits on how she would interfere in her life?* "Why? That's insane, Mom. You can't do that to people."

"If there's a man shtupping my daughter, I want to be damn sure that I will know as much as I can about him."

"Mother!"

"So, yes. His grandfather did evil—a Nazi, Eleanor. He is almost dead now. The private investigator's report says he does not have much time. The grandmother is dead. She died a long time ago."

"Did the grandmother know?" Eleanor asked, unable to contain her morbid curiosity.

"She wasn't German. And the PI thinks she was innocent based on the information he has. But who knows. This man showed up in Argentina after World War II. Changed his name as if that would take care of everything. Bah! And he was rich from war spoils, Eleanor. Blood money. From us. From our people."

Eleanor walked around to the front of the couch and sank down, her hands clutching each other. The shock was too much to bear. Daniel had told her his grandfather was--*What was the word he used? Ah, yes, he said his grandfather was reprehensible.* Eleanor had assumed he was abusive, verbally and possibly physically, but she had not envisioned anything of this nature. "What about Daniel? What about his parents?"

"The relation is through the father. It's his father's father. Daniel's mother Marietta gives an awful lot to charity. At least this depravity is through his father's line, not the mother's that we know of."

"Did anyone else in the family know?"

Her mother shook her head. "The PI didn't seem to think so. Daniel's father was a military officer in the Dirty War. I had never heard of it and started researching. The military killed so many people. They died with no names. It's in their bones, Eleanor--his father's, his grandfather's. This evil. You cannot deny this history. He will bring nothing but sorrow to our family. You cannot see Daniel again."

"The Daniel I know isn't that way," Eleanor said, a tight knot in her belly. "I'm not aware of what he's planning, but he mentioned he was doing something, changing something about his family."

"Lies. He has vile genes. And he is using the blood money from our people to further his own agenda. Who knows what he is capable of?"

"I cannot even believe I'm hearing this. You can't invade someone's privacy."

"I will do whatever it takes to make sure my daughter is safe. Your name means 'the light.' Don't bring darkness into our family."

The two women glared. The way she meddled with every single thing in her life never allowed anything to take shape. No guy Eleanor picked was ever good enough. She chose the wrong profession. Nothing she did was ever enough to make her mother proud.

"How did your date with Abraham go?" her mother asked.

This was just like her mom. Drop a huge dirty bomb and then change the subject.

Arguing with her did not work. Eleanor calmed herself with steady breathing, trying to find another way to communicate. Her mother stood there, so confident, so sure her version was accurate and the only way to look at the world. Eleanor wanted to tell her mother to leave, to lock the door behind her, and never speak to her again. But she loved her mom and wanted to find a way to work everything out.

"Mom," Eleanor tried, "do you not see what you're doing here? Daniel's life, his family history--none of it is your business."

"When he is with you I make it my business."

"Why are you so crazy!?" Eleanor shouted. Standing up, she threw the couch pillow onto the floor. It landed more softly than she would have liked, bouncing lamely off to one side. "Why won't you listen?"

"When I was younger," her mother said, cutting her off, "much younger, actually--I was only seventeen--there was a young man that I loved." She picked up the pillow and sat heavily on the couch. Looking out the window instead of directly at Eleanor, she smoothed the fabric, almost petting it like a cat.

The expression on her mother's face silenced Eleanor. She bit her lip and waited for her to continue. Her mother had never talked about anyone other than Tutti.

Her mother stared off into the distance as if remembering that time, and a half-smile crossed her face. "Oh, you should have seen him. He was wonderful. Charming and so, so handsome. He was a Gentile, too, and Nanna was furious," she added with a wry chuckle. "He had this little curl at the top, right here," she said, pointing to a place on her forehead, "and the bluest eyes I've ever seen. I was a teenager in love. So much in love." She sighed and closed her eyes. "But he wasn't who he said he was."

Her expression hardened. "He had lied. He was *Esbecja*--secret police, Polish KGB. I didn't know. Two weeks after I met him, my uncle disappeared. My aunt was found dead like a dog in the street. Both gone. I never see them again." Her eyes watered, but she didn't cry. She pinched her lips and looked away. "Nanna was never the same after that."

Eleanor's resolve softened. She sat next to her mother on the sofa but stopped short of putting an arm around her shoulders. She took her hand instead. "Mom, I'm sorry. I didn't know."

"Your Nanna and I never spoke of it again. I married a nice Jewish boy she picked out for me. He wasn't who I loved, but he was a kind, good man. After so many years, we found a certain kind of love."

"You didn't love Dad?" He and her mother had seemed the perfect couple. They never fought. They were in love, always hugging and smiling at each other.

"That's not what I said. But marriage isn't about

feelings. It's a business proposition. Besides, we were much older when we met."

"I can't even begin to think how . . . Is that why Grandma was cold to you? She was still mad about what happened?"

"There were other reasons. I don't want to discuss my story. This is about you, and I cannot let you go all crazy thinking you can love anyone. It doesn't work that way."

"How you made it through that . . . that kind of betrayal. How did you ever love Tutti?"

"It took a long time. Our relationship was based on mutual trust. Little by little, I learned to love again. But flaming passion burns out like a match. It has no business in marriage."

Eleanor tried to be as gentle as possible. "Daniel is not going to hurt me, not like that. He doesn't want to hurt me at all."

"You don't trust love! You *can't*," her mother said, her lip curling.

Eleanor lurched back as if her mother's words were an unseen missile. She took a deep breath and exhaled slowly, trying to put all this new information together in her head. Daniel was not his father or his grandfather. Learning her father and mother were not in love when they married surprised her. She'd always assumed that love came before marriage, even though her mother had negated that sentiment several times.

"I'm sorry you were hurt. Why didn't you tell me this before?"

"I never had to. And disrespect your father? Never. When I learned that visas are available, I stand in line for sixteen hours." She tossed the pillow back onto the couch. "The--oh, what is the word--the mafia types were paid to pull people out of line, but I pay them first. I am not blind anymore. We moved to America to get away. So poor. We were so, so poor, but we never take charity. No mafia. No soldiers banging on the door. Not once. Nothing else mattered." She moved to the mantle and straightened the pictures and candles. "I saw how they looked at us in America. I heard the words. Always Jew this, Jew that. But at least not to kill us. At least not to have secret police. Here we can be Jewish and live in peace. And you? You choose to deny this."

"Come with me. I will make you some tea."

Her mother scrunched her forehead as if she didn't trust Eleanor. Eleanor gingerly offered a hand, and her mother took it. "So, you see I must protect you, and here I can. I have information. This is why you cannot be with Daniel. His family is no good, which means he is no good."

She let go of Eleanor's hand and gathered her

purse and then followed her into the kitchen. She sat at the breakfast bar.

"We aren't in Poland anymore," Eleanor said. "Daniel is a good man, Mother." She wanted to push harder, to defend Daniel to the hilt, to call her mother out on her own hypocrisy of hiring a private detective, intimating that her mother was no better than the secret police. But that wouldn't be fair, either. Her mother was only trying to protect her daughter; she wasn't going to have Daniel thrown in prison. Whether she had no business or not, the truth was out.

"I know, little kitten, but--"

"You did it. You made our life here. You saved us."

Her mother's eyes grew big, and her mouth crumpled. She dropped her head into her hands. "So many people died, you know, whole villages were forced out. Families disappeared, gone. The anti-Zionist pogroms, what they did to us when I was young. We had to leave, but then we came back to find family. When things got better, and after I had you, especially, I did not want to stay and started planning. Then Tutti died, and there was nothing, no strings left. I didn't care how much things had changed in Poland. In my heart, nothing had changed. I had to get *you* out."

"We're here, Mom. We made it. We're alive."

Her mom sat up suddenly. She wiped the tears from her eyes. "Yes, we made it. Saturday we will go to

Temple. My daughter is with me. And we will walk there in peace, not in secret, not wondering…"

Eleanor nodded. She wanted to ask her mom to give Daniel a chance, to bless their dating, but now was not the time. And Daniel. What about Daniel? Did she tell him that she knew the truth about his grandparents? The truth about his parents? She could pretend she knew nothing about his family, but she did know. If they were to have a future she had to understand what he thought.

"When will you tell Daniel it's over?" her mother asked.

"He's a good man. He's trying to do something good. Please trust me."

Her mom stood suddenly, pounding both fists against the table. "Did you not hear anything I said?" She grabbed her purse and stomped away, slamming the front door behind her with a loud finality. The tea kettle whistled, and Eleanor didn't move, trying to comprehend what had just happened.

Chapter 21

The next morning, Eleanor awoke. Nothing felt solid anymore. The relationship with her mother was rocky. She didn't like the way she had handled the events with Daniel. But at least she had work to help keep her mind off current events. How come Daniel hadn't returned her last call? She wouldn't blame him, though, after her erratic behavior. But she hoped he'd call anyway. He did send flowers.

She quickly took a shower and dressed for the day in a pair of tan pants and a print silk blouse. She took her regular walking route to the office and got there with an hour to spare. She poured herself a coffee and sat at her desk.

She closed her eyes and tried to push out all the questions, all the thoughts. She wanted her mind to be quiet. She had a lot of work. The Vegas week was getting close. At her desk, she looked up her Polish history--the riots, the suppression of student protests, the mass migration of the Jewish population. From her benign and safe upbringing, she herself could never fully experience the raw violence that her mother had.

For that, she was thankful. She remembered snippets of the stories growing up, the somber words of disbelief and sadness. As time passed, the sadness from her mother faded. And what her family had experienced--the forced moves--how different it had been from her own childhood, thankfully. It seemed ludicrous she could have been killed for no other reason than being born Jewish. *People are funny. And horrible.*

A meeting reminder pinged, a bright sound in her somberness. She closed the websites and packed up her laptop. The meeting in the conference room was supposed to be one of the final reviews before Vegas. All-hands-on-deck as the congressman called it, so the key players to the Vegas trip would be attending. Madeline and Opal were already seated, speaking together in hushed tones. When she came in, they both looked at her.

"Eleanor? Are you okay?" asked Madeline. "You look awful."

"I am fine. Thank you for asking." She gave a hint of a smile. Of all the people who would notice something amiss, it would be Madeline. Nothing escaped her.

Opal lifted a sheaf of papers. "Eleanor, that research you did for me was perfect. I can't thank you enough."

"Oh, good, I am glad."

"My dad told me he wanted to talk to you about the seating-chart app. Have you heard from him yet?" Madeline asked.

"Not since our lunch." Eleanor checked her phone just in case. With all the hullabaloo with Daniel, her mother, and work, she might have missed it, but she found no new email or text from Louis.

Cheyenne and Katherine entered the room together talking with Chloe, who was right behind them.

"Hey, Eleanor," Cheyenne said, sitting next to her, "any updates on the kiss?"

Eleanor had her kiss but wasn't going to post it. The thrill was gone as was the desire to win. She clenched her jaw and held back her real thoughts about the game. The game was one more thing she didn't need. A game she didn't want to play. A childish game. She wanted to talk to Daniel first about his past. Daniel was not a game to her. It would hurt him if she posted a picture. There would be other job opportunities. Her app could sell. Her skills were excellent.

"No update. And you?" Eleanor felt relieved as if a burden had been lifted.

Cheyenne shrugged her shoulders. "We'll have to see, won't we?"

After everyone got settled, Katherine officially started the meeting by tapping her pen a few times against her metal to-go coffee cup. "I guess now is as good a time as any. I want all of you to know before the announcement." Kat waited until the women were turned to her, listening.

"Liz won't be returning to the office. Thankfully, the fiasco over the weekend with the Chinese Embassy hasn't hit the major papers yet, and Madeline will be handling that."

Eleanor asked Madeline, "What's going on with the Embassy? I'm out of the loop."

"I can fill you in later," replied Madeline, "but basically there was a shooting. Everyone is okay, and if I get more specifics I'll let you know."

"Opal," Kat said, continuing, "will be helping us manage the relationship with the Chinese to develop additional trade."

Katherine waited until the buzz settled before speaking. "This is it, ladies. We will have our winner officially tomorrow afternoon at 5 p.m. sharp. I'll announce it next week."

The meeting came to a close, and Eleanor walked

back to the office alone. Everyone else had meetings or other events to attend to. She would complete her onsite tasks then work from home the rest of the day.

Just as she sat down at her desk, her phone vibrated. She checked the message.

Daniel: Let's talk. Meet me at the Rhodeside Grill. Friday. Arlington. 7 p.m.

Eleanor's hands shook so hard she almost dropped the phone. Maybe there was a real chance between her and Daniel. Or maybe it was over.

Eleanor: Yes. Rhodeside Grill. 7 p.m.

Friday passed painfully slowly. The clock on her computer didn't seem to change. Eleanor seemed stuck in time. At 7 p.m., she was going to see Daniel again. What would she say to him? Her pragmatic imagination populated the conversation, and she cringed thinking of its words. She could only hope that whatever happened, it would turn out for the best.

BINGO was officially over on Friday, and the winner was going to be announced that afternoon. She worked to finalize the details to ensure a successful Vegas trip. How the team had managed to hide all the meeting preparations from the varying lobbyist groups boggled her mind. They'd had a few close calls apparently, but ultimately, the other shoe did not drop. The congressman and his chosen partner would be flying down to Vegas a few days after.

Eleanor didn't care who actually went with the congressman to Vegas. What did anything matter when you loved the wrong person? She wasted an hour clicking on various documents, trying to start a new project. Click. Close. Click. Close. Concentrating on work was impossible. Besides, no one was in the office. There was no point in staying.

Outside, the sky was blue, and white clouds bloomed along the horizon in a perfectly standard day. The street buzzed with cars driving by. The sidewalks were full of people walking to an unknown destination. The routine should have calmed her, but she felt at odds today. Nothing felt normal. She headed back to her townhome a little early to give herself a break from work and to relax before the upcoming evening with Daniel.

She put on a pair of jeans and a button-down print shirt paired with her Vans. She couldn't find her new sunglasses, so she settled for old ones. On her way out the door, she decided at the last minute to throw on a salmon-pink infinity scarf. She walked to the Metro. The late afternoon had cooled, so the walk was refreshing. Passing under a grove of cherry blossoms, she stopped to take a deep breath. The light scent of the flowers lifted her mood. Everything would work out.

She arrived at the bar before Daniel. The Rhodeside Grill was in Arlington. On the outdoor patio, people were having drinks, the atmosphere a festive Friday night one. Inside, the bar was fairly small. It was busy but not packed. The place had the look of a neighborhood bar, not modern but not old, either, with parquet flooring and wooden bar stools. There was a small stage set up for bands and a separate area for the restaurant.

She took a few minutes in the restroom to freshen up. The walk had warmed her skin, and she was ruddy in the cheeks. She straightened out her bangs with her fingers and took a deep breath before going back into the restaurant.

Daniel was now seated at the bar, stirring an amber drink. She paused to have a look at him. He hadn't seen her yet. He wasn't his usual jovial self. There was a somberness about him. Whatever was about to happen was going to happen, she thought, resigning herself to it. A part of her wasn't sure if she could be close to him without touching him, without wanting to run her hands through his unruly, dark curls.

He checked his watch and then turned toward her. She was startled into action and waved to him. He didn't smile, but he didn't frown, either. He gave her a kiss on each cheek. The smell of him assaulted her. She wasn't expecting her body to have such a strong reaction. He welcomed her to the chair next to him. Whatever was about to happen, she convinced herself that they would not part hating each other.

"How about a drink? Something stronger than beer?"

"I'll have what he's having," Eleanor told the bartender.

"Whiskey, neat."

The bartender brought up a clean glass from under the bar and poured two fingers. Daniel held his glass up but didn't say cheers. She clinked it in response, and they took a drink at the same time. The smooth liquid had a slight burn down her throat but settled warmly in her belly.

"Thank you for meeting me," Eleanor said. "I thought for sure that I would never see you again."

"The ambassador had the president-elect in town for fundraising, and we were expected to be on call. No phones were allowed because of media leaks."

"Ah." She slipped her hands on her knees. "I thought you didn't call for other reasons."

"No, I . . . There's so much to say. First, I want to apologize. I'm sorry if there was a misunderstanding about Valentina."

Eleanor apologized for her behavior as well. She told him she was sorry for acting so juvenile and that she was jealous. Daniel chuckled in response. But Eleanor felt uneasy. The more difficult conversation still remained. She needed to be brave and tell him.

"Jealous, hmm. The green-eyed monster?" There was a smile tugging at the corner of his lips. He was always the first to lighten the conversation.

"Yes, funny," she said. "Then I got my final kiss, but I did not post it. I wasn't sure what was going on . . . with us. I did not win BINGO. I mean, I could have. I had the kiss, but then I got your text."

"How did you get the final kiss?" he said, a bit terse in his question.

"My mother set me up on a date with a nice Jewish boy. I told you about him. We went out on Tuesday."

"How was the kiss?"

She wasn't expecting to hear that from him and could see he was concerned underneath his calm veneer. "It was a kiss. On the lips."

"A real kiss?"

Eleanor sat back, understanding his intention. Part of her wanted to make him jealous, too, the way she had felt when he was with Valentina. But she didn't want to play any more games. She had already played too many. "It was like kissing my brother."

She heard an audible sigh of relief. A tiny tingle

bounced in her belly, quick fingers of excitement trying to overwrite her exhaustion. "I'm so tired," she said. "This week was too much."

"Are you finished?" he asked, obviously feigning nonchalance.

"What do you mean?"

"Are you leaving now? Are you going home?"

"That's not what I meant," she said, her feelings taking a mercurial turn. "But I have to know, Daniel. Why did you want me to play that stupid game in the first place? Why were you trying to help me? Why did you want me to kiss other men?"

"I--" he stammered. "How do I say this?" He turned his chair and pulled hers toward him, so they were facing each other. The intensity of his gaze made her uncomfortable, but whatever he was about to tell her was truth.

"At first, I didn't *mind* if you played. I thought it was a game, a silly but harmless game. But then I did not know how strongly I would feel about you," he said.

Eleanor bit her lip and nodded. She felt the same way.

He took hold of her hands. "At first, I thought it would be fun to help you. But after that night, after our kiss, everything changed. You are not like the others, so fluffy and bouncy and full of shit. Eleanor you are *la verdad de la milanesa*. Literally this means the truth of the Milanese. In Argentina, this is how we say you are the real deal. Eleanor, you are the real thing." He paused to lift his pendant. "You feel like this, like home to me."

The room filled with people coming in for happy hour but to her there was only him.

He grasped the barstool arms and pulled her closer. Then he leaned toward her, close to her face, almost near enough to touch her nose but not quite. "I don't want you to ever kiss another man but me."

Eleanor felt a jolt of electricity zing through her body. She moved her hands up his arms, across his biceps, and stopped at his shoulders. "And if you ever want me to kiss anyone else, I will never speak to you again."

"Never." He leaned forward, placed his hands on her cheeks and kissed her. "Never."

His lips against hers where they belonged set her core on fire. But the hardest conversation was yet to come. Was he a man willing to risk the wrath of her mother? She rubbed his cheek and then pulled away to let him know the movement was done out of necessity, not rejection. "There is more we need to discuss."

"I see. What else is there?"

She glanced around the bar crowded with people laughing and the general din of revelry. "Not here."

"Let's go to my place." He stood and took her hand and led her outside. She had no idea where he lived, but she trusted him. They caught a cab and headed back into the city to a neighborhood between Dupont Circle and Adams Morgan. His building looked newer, modern. "I rent this place. The embassy is close by, so I can walk."

Once inside his apartment, she couldn't miss a large oil painting above his couch. Two gauchos sat astride their horses looking over the Argentine pampas, or plain. The apartment also held the reality of an athletic young man. A pair of soccer shoes were clumped in one corner with dried dirt clods spotting the floor. A hook from the ceiling held a mountain bike with some serious shocks. An abandoned tennis racket lay on the kitchen table. In the living room was an ultra-modern leather couch. A sleek metal and glass coffee table held a few books of poetry by Pablo Neruda.

"It is good to see you again," he said, brushing his lips against her cheek. "I missed you." He smelled good, like fresh mountain air and bergamot.

She raised an eyebrow at him. "I like your books," she said, walking over to the built-in shelves near the couch. Books crammed every inch of space—in some cases they were double stacked.

"I was at the grocery store a few days ago. I am going to make you something special. Just for you."

Eleanor murmured a yes but stayed focused on the books, running her fingers over the older ones. "These look special."

"They are. Those are from my grandfather. I . . . I'm not sure if I should keep them." He waved her into the kitchen.

She was about to follow him in. Part of her wanted to let it go, to respect Daniel's privacy. But she would wonder then about the knowledge her mother had uncovered, and that wonder would eat a hole in her. They should be having a serious conversation. "First we need to talk."

"What is it, *galgita?* What is so important?"

"It's about your grandfather and your dad. The thing is . . . I know."

Daniel's shoulders went stiff. "What is it you know or think you know?"

"That your grandfather was a Nazi," she said distinctly, carefully enunciating the words as if that would help give her clarity.

"Ah, yes, my grandfather." He relaxed his body and met her gaze with a sense of fierceness. "Come with me into the kitchen. It is a long story, and it calms me to cook." He waved her into the kitchen.

She followed him in. His kitchen had dark wood

cabinets and granite countertops. She sat on a stool at the breakfast bar.

He went to the fridge and pulled out green peppers and a paper bag, setting them on the counter, and then pulled out an onion and spices from the pantry and placed them next to the peppers. "I'm going to make fajitas." From the paper bag, he pulled out two containers. One was leftover chicken. He placed it in a pan to warm it up. "And would you cut up the onions and the peppers in strips?" he asked.

"That's easy enough," she said. He handed her a knife and cutting board. She stood and took the peppers, rinsing them off first.

Daniel put an iron skillet on and added olive oil. "My grandfather was a Nazi. I found out about him in school. Some kid taunted me about him being German, and well, it was something people knew. Parents would never say anything but kids, you know, nothing is off the table."

"So what happened? Did you ask your dad? Your grandfather?" Eleanor asked as she cut the vegetables into slices.

Daniel got out another cutting board and knife. With a ripe tomato in hand, he paused. "My grandfather---Granpapi---is dying. I asked him about it with the directness of a schoolboy. When I was little, I had no idea what it meant to be a 'Nazi,' only that it was terrible. No one wanted to talk about it. I asked at the dinner table, and it was like the air was sucked out of the room."

Eleanor had finished cutting up the onions and peppers and laid her knife down. Her heart ached for him. How difficult that must have been for him to find out. He picked up her board and slid the vegetables into the hot pan, the peppers sizzling when they hit the hot oil. He added a dash of spices. With a deep breath, he continued. "You see, my mother's family is Argentinian, but our ancestors came from Italy many generations ago. My mother, she tells me our ancestors immigrated because they were so poor they were dying of hunger." He turned to look at her. "A story that is similar to your family's."

She met his eyes. They were expressive, hopeful, and sincere. Daniel broke her gaze and stirred the food when the pan smoked. Eleanor went to the fridge. She pulled out a bottle of white wine. He pointed to the cupboard, and she opened it to find wine glasses. She poured the wine and handed him one. "You didn't know any of this?"

"To me he was a sweet old man, kind to a fault, full of good humor. I learned about my grandfather when I was eight, maybe nine. Even in Argentina they teach how evil the Nazis were. I buried my shame and confusion deep. My granpapi a Nazi? I could not reconcile the two images. How could someone so loving be one of them?"

She chopped the parsley and tomatoes. "Did he ever make amends?"

Daniel poured black beans into a pan. *He really does cook. He wasn't just showing off earlier.* No one else had ever cooked for her, not any one of her mother's hand-picked Jewish boys.

"My grandfather? Not directly. He has mild dementia. The nurse says he wants to die but then he is terrified. He keeps begging for forgiveness, but," Daniel paused, looking away, "no one can give him the forgiveness he wants."

"So it stops there?"

"No." Daniel sipped his wine. "It gets worse. Are you sure you want to hear this?" he asked, fingering his medallion. "It is a painful thing that I have been living with this last year."

She reached across the table, clasping her hands over his. "You're a good man, Daniel. Out with it."

"I think I was stolen from my real parents," he said, his eyes forlorn. "I'm afraid that Mrs. Marietta Prado is not my biological mother."

"What?" Eleanor asked. "How did ... what makes you think that?"

"Where do I start?" he asked rhetorically. He stirred the chicken and then turned off the gas burner.

"I'll begin with my father. I didn't learn the truth about him until my late twenties." He turned the burner off the hot onions and peppers. He got out two plates and set tortillas on them. "Papi had a cold temper, brutal and hard. Mama had the stereotypical fiery Latin passion. Their arguments were legendary."

Eleanor murmured, enough to let him know that she was listening but not enough to interrupt.

He prepared the tortilla by adding a handful of shredded cheese. "He worked for the military, a good job then. But years later, I began to learn about the Dirty War."

"And what was that?" she asked, somehow knowing the importance of this topic, how the knowledge would change their relationship.

"During the military junta people disappeared. Gone. Like your aunt and uncle in Poland." He paused to look at her. "I was contacted by this group called the Grandmothers of the Plaza. They help reunite the lost babies, the ones who were taken from their parents with their families."

"The parents who were killed by the military? You think you are one of those babies?" she asked.

"Yes. The military junta in Argentina ended in 1983. They killed and tortured so many people. Fathers and mothers disappeared and many of the babies were placed within military families. There is no documentation. Those responsible believed if they didn't leave a trace, no one would know."

"Why do you think you are one of them?"

"I was born the last year of the war. My parents are military, my dad . . . I don't know exactly what he did, but it's not good."

"You think he stole you from a family and raised you as his son?"

"That would mean my parents were murdered. I don't want to think that. But . . . the facts. I have my reasons." Daniel placed his head in his hands.

"Oh, Daniel. I'm so sorry."

"I'm trying to fix it. My mom has old work files from my father. I don't know exactly what is in them, probably nothing, but I want them transferred to the Grandmothers of the Plaza."

"It seems such a small act. How is she taking it?"

"Not well, but there is hope. I am very close to convincing her." He made the rest of the fajita by adding the peppers and onion, chicken, tomatoes and parsley with a dollop of sour cream and chimichurri. He handed her a finished plate.

She rolled the tortilla and took a bite. The flavors blended in a way that none were lost. The tang of the chimichurri smoothed over the smoky flavors of the beans. But she wished the food didn't taste so good— she dreaded hearing the rest of his story.

"Good food feeds an empty heart," he said as if reading her mind. "That's what Mama always says to me. There was so much sadness in our family." He set the fajita down.

Eleanor sat back. "What's next?"

"What do you mean?" he asked tersely.

"You are aware of my history," she said quietly. "My grandmother was nearly killed by the likes of your Granpapi. What do you plan to do?"

Daniel pushed his chair back and jumped up. "What do you mean, what am *I* going to do? I can't fix everything. I can't go back. I can't undo *anything*. It's not my fault."

Eleanor wanted to react, but it would only flame the fires of frustration. "All I meant is what is next for you? How do you find out if you are one of the lost babies? Are you taking a genetic test? Or will you ignore it? Will she hand over the boxes?"

"If I hand over the documents my family could lose our reputation. If I take the test my mother's last son may be lost to her." Daniel paced through the kitchen, rounding the island and then back to her with his feet in an aggressive stance, his arms crossed. "But I am going to ruin my family. I'm taking the test. I want my mom to release my father's old files. I will break the curse."

"I'm sorry you have to do this," Eleanor said, calm

in the face of his anger. She took his hands in hers. "It's the right thing to do. Tell me more about this so-called curse." If anything, maybe she could help him break through this bit of superstition.

His shoulders relaxed, and he circled his head around stretching out his neck. "I remember this gypsy. I don't remember much, just a lot of dark cloth and long black hair. I was young, but I can't forget her words. She said there was a curse on the family."

"What do you mean? Like a blood curse?" They had finished eating, and she took his hand to lead him into the living room so they could sit more comfortably.

"I don't know. But both my siblings died less than a year later. Mama freaked out. Papi got a job at the embassy. We left the country, and she's never gone back."

"My mother was like that, too," Eleanor said. "Once we left Poland, she never went back."

"It's a lot, no?"

"My mother knows who you are and about your family. I'm embarrassed and ashamed to tell you this."

"How?"

"She hired a private investigator," Eleanor said, closing her eyes. "I have a hard time understanding the depths she will go to. She wants me to quit seeing you. She's certain you're going to break my heart."

"Do you believe her?"

"I wouldn't be here if I did. In fact, she is mad at me for this," Eleanor said, moving her hands back and forth between them, "because I wanted to talk to you."

He ran his hands through his hair. "Did she really hire a private investigator? She is very determined, isn't she? I would have told all this to you willingly. There was no need to go to such extremes."

"I am angry about it, but . . . she is my mother, Daniel. It was her way of protecting me."

"By hurling my family history between us? We are not our parents or our grandparents, Eleanor. I am not like my father or my grandfather. Please tell me you understand this."

Their eyes locked, hers seeking, his determined but open and begging.

"I believe you, Daniel. I wouldn't have come if I didn't know you are different."

"What do you want, Eleanor?"

"What do you mean? I'm here, aren't I?"

"Is that going to be enough? Will you defend me against your mother?"

Eleanor creased her eyebrows. If she was going to be with Daniel it meant she had to be true to herself. And what did she want? It was a question she had left unanswered even though she had already made choices. Now it was really a matter of saying it aloud, of acknowledging the truth of how she wanted to live. Acknowledging it in front of him.

"I will defend you, Daniel. You. I want you. This. I've wanted something different in my life for a long time. But I never did anything about it. I had no idea what I was looking for until I met you. I feel free when we're together."

He reached for her hand. "I feel a sort of respite when I am with you, too. Like I am standing in the sun after being in the rain for too long. Come here, you," he said, his deep voice simmering. He placed his hands around her waist, curling her in. "A kiss for the chef?"

He brought her in closer, and his heart pounded against hers. "After I make you this food, you know what will happen, yes?"

"Do tell."

"You will forever be swayed by my charms and the sound of my voice," he said and nuzzled her neck with his chin. He stood. Eleanor let him pull her off the sofa and into a hug. He held onto her as if she were the only thing in the world. They walked to his bedroom, Daniel in the lead. His room was a cross between decadent and utilitarian. Luscious velvet curtains paired with a plain, white down comforter. He took off her shirt and unclasped her bra. She helped unbutton his shirt and unbuckled his belt. Their eyes never left each other, his hands warming her back, rubbing her shoulders.

"I want you next to me."

She took off her pants but left on her underwear. He did the same. She slipped into the bed, and he climbed in beside her.

"I don't know how I would face this without you," he said, pulling her into a spoon position and wrapping his arms around her, their bodies melding into one. "You make me brave."

Eleanor smiled and rubbed his forearm. "Together, we are strong."

There was a small voice in the back of her mind that needed to ask him about his religion, to find out if he was serious about being Catholic and what it meant to him, the last hurdle between them. But they had already traversed through such intense territory she didn't feel it was the right time to bring it up.

Chapter 23

Marietta Prado had gotten the call at 4:32 a.m. on Saturday morning. The nurse spoke clearly and calmly in Spanish. *Senor Prado esta muerte.* At first, Marietta did nothing. She lay in her bed with her eyes open. One man's life had ended. She thought of all the lives he had touched and all the new paths forced because of him. *May purgatory be hell on your soul.* Death was all around her. It was the reason she had left Argentina, a place that seemed as vital to her as the blood that flowed through her body. And yet, she hadn't been back to Argentina in almost twenty years.

Perhaps her husband never had a chance. He had grown up in the shadows of Granpapi, who gave lessons in violence and cold logic. All the lives he had changed. Lucas, her husband, was a good man, a good father, but he had the old German's unyielding rationality, even when he was angered. A complex man, he was fiercely protective of his children and yet so stony with others. He worked hard. He was gone constantly, so their children had been raised with her temperament. But only Daniel was left. In her bed, she crossed herself.

Daniel was alive, though. Did she believe that old gypsy's curse? If so, why had he been spared? She had believed enough to move out of Argentina and never go back. And now Daniel wanted his papi's old work boxes. Maybe she would give him all of them. Maybe she'd give him one--the year of his birth: 1983.

She wished she could wake up naive, uninformed, unhinged by knowledge. She was too hot suddenly, the blankets smothering. She tossed off the covers. The morning air was chilly, and she walked to the bathroom. After a shower, she dried her hair and then stood in front of her closet.

What does one wear when planning to betray the memory of a husband? Of a family?

Something nice. She picked out a pair of white pants, the crease deep along the middle of the leg, and paired it with something dark and plain and then put on a light cardigan.

In the kitchen, Marietta sipped her yerba mate, a form of Argentine coffee, while looking over the Japanese maples and Virginia oak trees that had been planted to make a natural border around her backyard. Beyond that were acres of rolling hills primarily used for grazing and horse trails. Her son was right, but she hadn't been ready to admit it. The past needed to be free. She needed to let it go. Granpapi was dead now.

In her stocking feet, she padded across the tile to put her shoes on by the back door. Outside, the air was chillier. She pulled her sweater in closer as she hurried to the barn. In the tack room, back in the corner, the 1983 box was under the horse blankets. She'd taken it back out there after Daniel had left the other day.

Marietta planned to uncover them but didn't want to smudge her white pants. She looked around the tack room and found a clean barn jacket. She put it on and then identified the box she would give Daniel. After all these years, it was time to give it to him.

She carried the container to her car where she set it on the ground and took off the jacket, placing it on the back seat before putting the box on top of it. Then she returned to the house for another cup of yerba mate to calm herself. Did she have any restrictions about the information in the box, or would she let Daniel do as he wished? She'd prefer no media coverage, but she was realistic enough to know she could not control the future.

After finishing her drink, she returned to the car. The clock on the dashboard read 7:45. She thought about calling Daniel to tell him she was coming, but she might lose her will if she did.

Chapter 24

*R*ebekah Winslow was an early riser. She had always been a night owl as a young girl, but adult responsibilities had cured her of staying up late and replaced it with waking early. In Poland, it was her job to gather the eggs in the morning, her responsibility to find secretarial work which paid practically nothing, and everywhere try to avoid harassment from anyone who considered her beneath them.

Her daughter was lucky to have even the basics of a childhood. She was lucky to have the opportunities that she had in America—college, a good job, even if she wasn't a lawyer. But Rebekah felt her daughter wasn't appreciative or really even aware of those opportunities. That was why Rebekah had to do everything in her power to assure her daughter didn't mess up her life.

She would not leave that to chance. After leaving Eleanor on Wednesday night, they hadn't spoken again. When Eleanor refused to break up with Daniel, Rebekah had contacted the PI who had dug up information on Daniel and instructed him to call regarding Eleanor's movements anywhere besides work and her townhome.

Saturday morning, she woke early and checked her phone. The battery had died. She grunted in frustration. After she plugged it in, she saw ten missed calls, six messages, and two text messages. Eleanor had gone to meet Daniel on Friday. Rebekah's phone was pressed against her ear. The private investigator was on the other end of the line. He informed her that Eleanor and Daniel were together, and she had spent the night at his house.

Bile rose in Rebekah's mouth. After leaving Poland and all the hate she had endured, she couldn't believe someone like Daniel and his family had resurfaced in America to be involved with Eleanor. Daniel and his family were bad blood, of that she was certain. She had to nip this in the bud.

The PI cleared his throat, and she was brought back to their conversation. She had no further instructions for him. After she hung up, she ground her teeth. She didn't like mistakes. She liked them even less when she made one herself. But sometimes technology got the better of her.

I told Eleanor not to do this. Why didn't she listen?

Once clean and coiffed, she stood in front of her closet. What did one wear for confrontation? Something presentable, something she might wear to a formal tea at the consulate, conservative but matronly. She chose a pair of black pants and a stiffly ironed light-blue cotton shirt. That should do it.

She had no prepared speech for Daniel, but her words would keep Eleanor safe. She only cared that her baby not be hurt by that man. In the end survival and safety were what mattered. A life well lived? Bah, who had time for that? She put on a light jacket and tied the belt snug and tight. The wall clock said 7:50. At a decent pace, she'd be able to walk to Daniel's by 8:30.

$\mathcal{E}$leanor woke as a car revved in the distance, something with an old-fashioned V-8 engine. Someone was in a hurry somewhere, she thought, glad she didn't have to get up. She snuggled into the soft sheets, and Daniel grunted and put his arm around her. It was Saturday. Saturday! She bolted upright, found a folded T-shirt from a laundry pile and ran downstairs to find her cell. She had to let her mom know she wouldn't be able to make Shabbat. She checked the time. It was eight, and her mother always showed up at eight-thirty for the nine o'clock service.

The call rang, but no one picked up, so Eleanor left a brief message. Hopefully, her mother wouldn't knock on her door this morning and wonder why she wasn't home. Eleanor sighed. She'd deal with the fallout later. Right now, a nice lazy morning snuggling with Danny seemed a perfect way to spend her time.

In the kitchen, she poured herself a glass of water. How was she going to resolve this? How was she going to keep seeing Daniel when her mother was so paranoid? There was only one answer: She had to take a stand for Daniel, outcome be damned. She took the glass of water up to his room, removed her T-shirt and slipped back into bed.

"Where'd you go, *galgita*?" he asked as he brought her into his embrace.

"Today is Saturday. I had to call my mom to tell her I wasn't going to Shabbat."

"Oh," he said, uncomprehending. A look of confusion crossed his face. He sat up. "Do I need to go?"

"Sleepyhead, this is your house." He settled back, and she curled next to him under the sheet.

He gave her a quick kiss. "I thought for a moment we were at your house."

"Thankfully no. We don't have to worry about my mother knocking on your door. I left her a voice mail."

"What are we going to do?" he asked. "We can't live our lives sneaking around behind her back."

"The only thing she will accept is if you convert to Judaism and promise to circumcise yourself," Eleanor said with a half chuckle. She was joking, but when she said the words, she realized they were true.

"Circumcise myself? Wouldn't proclaiming my undying love be enough?" He rubbed his hand over her shoulder, down the curve of her waist, and ended with a small pat on her bottom.

The doorbell rang. Daniel sat up again. "Who is that? That can't be your mom, can it?"

Eleanor shook her head. Three knocks followed. He put on a pair of boxers and jeans before heading down. She admired his chest and arms, the nice biceps.

She heard him thump down the stairs and waited, listening with a sudden feeling of dread.

DANIEL RAN DOWN THE STAIRS, the air cold against his feet. The person had to be the newspaper boy. Or maybe it was his nosy neighbor from Greece who always liked to check in on him and then proceeded to tell the rest of the building his business, even if she did make up for it with her incredible desserts. He flung the door open only to find his mother standing in front of the door.

"Mama? What are you doing here?"

She held a box in her hands. One of *the* boxes. His jaw dropped.

"Are you going to let me in? It's not exactly warm out here."

He stepped aside to let her in. "Why are you here?" He couldn't take his eyes off the box clearly labeled 1983.

"Granpapi has died this morning at the *estancia*." She said it without emotion.

Daniel took the box from her and placed it on the coffee table. He gestured her to the couch.

"That *man* is finally dead, and I couldn't go back to sleep."

"Are you going back to Argentina? Will you tell Papi?"

"I suppose you and I should go back. There is the reading of the will, and even though he doesn't deserve it we must bury him. And no, I'm not telling Papi. He wouldn't remember anyway. But I wanted to give you this," she said, placing her hand on the box and tapping it lightly. "I thought about making sure certain names were kept out of the media, but what do I care? I'm an old woman. I don't even see those people any--"

A single sharp rap sounded. Daniel and his mom exchanged confused glances before he got up to open the door.

Rebekah Winslow stood looking as if she were the devil himself on fire. "Where is she? What have you done with her?" She brushed past him.

"Mrs. Winslow? What are you doing here?" Daniel asked, following her into the living room.

"I told my daughter to stay away from you." She looked from Daniel to Mama and focused on her. "From you and your disgusting family. How do you live with yourself? Knowing what your husband and father-in-law did?"

"Excuse me?" Marietta replied, rising from the couch and moving closer. "You don't even know who I am."

"I know all about you and your family. You should be ashamed."

"Mrs. Winslow, meet my mother, Señora Prado," Daniel said, not knowing what else to say.

Rebekah directed her eye-piercing gaze back to him. Her shoulders squared, and her chin thrust out. "How dare you shtup my daughter? That is disgusting. You don't deserve her."

Marietta stood next to Daniel, her hands on her hips. "Don't you dare talk to my son that way. You need to leave. I don't know what gives you the *cojones* to talk to my son that way, but it stops. Now. Or I'll call the police."

ELEANOR THREW her clothes on and rushed downstairs, taking two steps at a time, and launched herself into the living room. "Mother!" she called out before anyone could continue the argument. She half-bowed toward Daniel's mother. "Mrs. Prado, it's nice to meet you. I'm sorry. I'll explain everything to her."

"Explain what? Her rude manners? Who are you?" Marietta asked, looking to Daniel.

Rebekah Winslow stamped her heel and turned to Eleanor. "Enough of this. We are leaving. Don't bother saying goodbye, Daniel. Don't ever contact Eleanor again, or I'll put a restraining order against you."

"Mom, stop. It's not what you think."

"It's exactly what I think. It's obvious. He's taking advantage of you." Rebekah paused to look him up and down with disdain.

"No one is leaving until I get answers," said Marietta Prado, her arms crossed. "Daniel? What is the meaning of this? Who is this girl?"

"This is my new girlfriend, Eleanor. She's a Polish Jew."

"A Polish Jew? Is that how you introduce people?" retorted Mrs. Winslow.

Rebekah took hold of her daughter's elbow and moved to the door.

Daniel stepped toward Rebekah with his hands out. "Please, stop, Mrs. Winslow. Don't leave. Your daughter is the one who helped me to do the right thing." He turned to his mama. "Eleanor is the one who helped me realize why we need the box and why we must give it to the Grandmothers of the Plaza. I didn't want the introduction to go this way, but well, as you can see here we are."

Mrs. Winslow straightened her shirt collar and pulled down the front of her jacket. "I don't care about any stupid box. Eleanor, get your shoes and coat. We are leaving."

Eleanor pulled her arm from her mother's grasp. "Enough. You have to listen."

"I know who they are. I don't need the whole story. I know exactly what kind of people they are. Nazi scum. Killers." She stomped out the front door.

Eleanor crossed her arms and refused to go. She was tired of Mama's anger. Tired of her always having to be right. She had promised herself she would stick up for Daniel, and if it meant not running after her mother, so be it. She wanted to move next to Daniel, but she was shocked still, breathing hard from the adrenaline coursing through her body. She stood awkwardly in front of Marietta and glanced at the box. "I am so sorry, Mrs. Prado."

Marietta grasped Eleanor's hand. A look of compassion crossed her face. "I am a mother, too. Go after her. It's the right thing to do."

Chapter 26

Daniel watched as the front door shut behind Eleanor. He turned to look at his mama.

Her arms were crossed, and a stern look was on her face. "Daniel, you have some explaining to do. I've half a mind to pick up this box and go home and burn it."

"Mama, please. Come into the kitchen. I can make you coffee and--"

"I'm not here for a social visit, *mijo*." She tapped the box with her foot.

"Come into the kitchen and sit. I have your favorite beans and that creamer you like so much."

"One cup of coffee." She followed him into the kitchen. "It's coming to light, isn't it?"

His mother paused in front of the family pictures. In one, he was seven and smiling proudly on the back of a brown horse with a white star. Granpapi had taken the picture. Next to it was an old and worn picture, framed, of his family before Thomas and Camila had died. He and his siblings were blissfully unaware of what was to come. There were other family pictures of just him and his parents, but he kept those in his bedroom.

"I miss Thomas and Camila," Marietta said wistfully. "I hope they are waiting for me up there." She crossed herself.

"I do, too," he said, taking her hand and leading her into the kitchen.

"I always thought the right thing to do was to just ignore the past, to leave it behind. How does that woman know about Granpapi?"

Daniel pushed a button to start coffee brewing and got a ceramic cup out of his cupboard.

Marietta sat down at the breakfast bar. She rubbed the side of her neck. "What is going on, *mijo*? I came here to give you the box, but now ... I do not know if I can give it to you after that woman's vitriol."

Daniel opened the fridge and brought out the cream. He set it down and stroked his chin, thinking first about how he wanted to tell his mama. "When I met Eleanor and she told me about her family's past, I realized I had never met anyone impacted by someone like Granpapi.

And her mother's life sounded similar to those of the people who had lived through the Dirty War. Everything changed for me. I felt so protective of her. Eleanor made me realize we can't hide from the truth anymore."

He took a pan out and heated up the cream.

Marietta nodded. "Love has a way of making people do the things they always should have done." She turned to look into the living room. "For a long time that box scared me. That's why I never touched it."

"Do you know what is in the boxes?" The coffee had finished brewing enough for a cup. He poured the cream into the cup first and then filled the rest with coffee and handed it to her.

"No, I don't," she sighed and took a sip. "You make the best coffee, *mijo*."

He smiled in recognition of the compliment. When he looked at her, she seemed tired, yet the tense lines were gone from her expression. She appeared to be at peace finally.

"I know they are work papers. I only thought they were important because Papi kept the boxes all these years. He reacted so strongly about them I believed they had to be protected at any cost." Her eyes widened in the moment of realization. "In marriage sometimes you make these assumptions. You think you know a person so well when really it is a misunder-standing."

"Should we look in the box first?" he asked. "Clarify anything so you won't be surprised?"

Marietta's gaze returned to the living room as she appeared to consider the request. "No. Let the Grand-mothers do that. I don't think anything will surprise me."

He rubbed his hands on his jeans and then wrung his hands together. "You know that Eleanor is Jewish."

"I gathered as much. Your Granpapi would have cared. Your father too. I would have cared a long time ago. But I am not them. I make my own choices now. Who you are with is up to you."

He felt he could breathe again. The tight feeling in his chest dissipated.

"But I have to warn you," she said, pointing at him, "if you get married and have children, love is what will get you through the hard parts. Be sure you have that."

"I understand, Mama." He gathered his courage with a deep breath. "I still plan on taking the DNA test that The Grandmothers of the Plaza have requested."

Marietta sat up straight. "Ah. You still have questions?"

Daniel was about to reply, but she interrupted him.

"Wait." She met his eyes without hardness, regret or sadness. Instead he saw understanding and affection. "I know the truth of *you*. Take the DNA test if you must." She waved her hand as if declaring the DNA test was akin to an annoying fly.

"I will always be your son." Daniel swallowed. He poured himself a cup of coffee to steady his hand.

"Look at me."

He set the coffee pot down and met his mama's eyes.

"Do you know why I named you Daniel?"

"No, Mama." Daniel held the handle of his coffee cup and rested his thumb against the warm ceramic as a way to calm his beating heart.

"You are the strong one, a lion. I knew you would bring light into our family. I couldn't do it. I was too scared."

"Don't worry, Mama. It will be okay." He came around the kitchen island and put his arms around her.

She kissed him on the cheek and rubbed the spot with her hand. "I am so proud of you. You are stronger than I could ever be."

Chapter 27

*E*leanor had caught up to her mother at the Metro entrance. Silence lay between them. Eleanor knew she had to talk to her mother, but she wasn't sure what the right words were or how to say them. Her throat felt tight, closed off. At Eleanor's townhome, Mama sat on the gray minimalistic couch. She didn't sit back and try to relax. Her knees were together but not crossed. Her lips were pressed together. She was a matriarch made of steel.

Eleanor started toward the kitchen. She didn't want to speak to her mother, but old habits kicked in. She turned and asked, "Would you like something to drink? I can make a cup of coffee? I have some of the Jasmine tea you like."

"No, thank you," she said. Her lips remained staunchly pinched.

This relationship as it stood needed to end. Eleanor felt like she was going to explode. How could she talk to her? What were the right words to unlock her severity? "I can't keep doing this," she said. "Being polite and pretending everything is okay. The way you treated Daniel and his mother this morning was shameful."

"My daughter's safety is paramount. That is all that matters," she said, refusing to meet Eleanor's glare.

"We don't live in Poland anymore. Daniel is a good man. You're acting like the *Esbecja*."

Mama reacted as if Eleanor had slapped her. "If you are going to win over my heart, Eleanor, and change my mind, this is not the way."

"What is the way then? I've tried asking nice. I've tried being logical. But what can I say to you?"

Mama's expression softened as she thought about the question.

"I love you, Mother, and I want us to have a good relationship, but I don't know if I can follow your life plan for me. I want to choose who I love."

Her mother stayed still on the couch and didn't say anything for what seemed a long time. She gave a slight shrug. "I will think about it. I can't change my ways, my past, simply because you ask."

Eleanor nodded. "It's a start, though." She was still

processing the last twenty-four hours, but she needed to be alone to organize her thoughts before expressing them to her mother. "I'm going to take a shower. Then we can talk."

In the bathroom, she looked in the mirror. The beginnings of a smile appeared as she formulated a plan. It was risky and mildly underhanded but nothing her mother hadn't already done to her. Then she sent Daniel a text. If her plan was to succeed, she needed him. After scrubbing herself, Eleanor felt clean and lighter in spirit. She put on something that made her feel brave and strong--a pair of light corduroy pants and a crisp shirt. Everything was in place. And in the next fifteen minutes, hopefully, her mother would see reason too.

Eleanor went downstairs to see if her mother had moved to the kitchen yet. Eleanor liked to clean when she was stressed, but her mother liked to bake. Preferably something with yeast so she could beat down the dough, but Eleanor's kitchen was devoid of any yeast.

"Eleanor, I'm in the kitchen. Come here, please."

When her mother was polite, her anger simmered just under the surface. The more polite she was the more fire she unleashed. But Eleanor was ready. She knew her mother was ready to talk, ready to consider change. Even so, her plan was in place. Her shoulders squared, she stood up tall. She had learned well from Rebekah Winslow. Two could play this game.

In the kitchen, her mother had rolled up her sleeves and put on an apron. On the counter was a package of dried yeast, flour, and dried onions. Eleanor hadn't realized she had the ingredients in her kitchen. Her mother was sifting flour into a bowl. She was making bialys. The recipe had been handed down from generation to generation for more than a hundred years.

Eleanor came in and poured herself a glass of water and checked her watch. It wouldn't be long until her plan unfolded. "I'm going to make tea. Would you like a cup?" She brought out an electric teapot from her cupboard and filled it with water.

"Yes. I know this recipe by heart," her mother said. "I taught you how to make this when you were a little girl."

"I know the recipe by heart, too." She flipped the power switch on the kettle.

"Then you'll know that no one has changed the ingredients since its creation. I don't know why you use that thing. Just boil it on the stove."

"This is faster and uses less electricity. And you are making this with a cake of yeast that was purchased at a store. I highly doubt anyone had Fleischmann's packets of active dry yeast available a hundred years ago." The water had started to boil. The sound of furious bubbles was in the air.

"That's not the point."

Eleanor put her hands on her hips. "That is the point. Things are different. Times have changed. Daniel is not the kind of man who hurt you in Poland."

"He is a Catholic who comes from bad blood." Mama made a well in the flour and added the water, after which she stirred the ingredients with a fork.

"Are you going to treat him the way you were treated? You are going to judge him based on his people? That's so hypocritical."

Mama pounded the counter with the flats of her hands. Little puffs of flour radiated in a starburst pattern around them. "How dare you? How dare you insinuate I am anything like him or his wretched family."

"How dare I? You haven't even given him a chance. You don't know anything about what he is doing."

"I am sure he is doing nothing. They ran away, Eleanor. His grandfather ran away like a coward. His parents moved here. Always they escape."

Eleanor refused to give in. She held a cup between them. "Daniel was only eleven or twelve when they moved. He had no say. Just like I had no say when we moved to America."

Mama took the cup and set it down on the counter. "These people," she said quietly, "it is in the blood. He is no different. I am saving you from a man who can only break your heart."

"You're not." Eleanor said. "Please listen to me."

There was a knock at the door, and Mama's eyes narrowed. Eleanor started toward it.

"Don't answer it."

"Listen to him. Hear what he has to say. That's all I ask. If you don't agree then send him away."

Mama agreed with the barest of nods.

Eleanor went to the front door. She paused with her hand on the doorknob. She put all her faith in Daniel, praying he could explain everything to her mother's satisfaction. If he didn't and her mother told him to leave, what then? She'd have to keep trying. She'd try to break the cycle of prejudice and past.

Opening the door, Daniel stood there with a box in his hands. As he came in, he gave her two quick kisses on the cheek. "We will be fine, *galgita*," he whispered in her ear. "I promise. Where is she?"

"In the kitchen. That's where she feels at home."

He stopped when he reached the doorway to the kitchen. He and Mama stared at each other. Mama raised her eyebrows as if to acknowledge his presence, but her expression remained skeptical.

"As you know, my grandfather was a Nazi who

escaped from Germany." Daniel started right in without any basic pleasantries. "He took on the surname Prado, and no one cared. There were no databases or extensive rules about names back then."

Mama scrunched her shoulders and crossed her arms. She had finished mixing the ingredients and laid a kitchen towel over the top, setting the bowl to the side to let the dough rise.

Daniel walked in and placed the box on a clear part of the countertop. "I don't know what he did, but it must have been horrible. Anyway, my mother came to tell me this morning that he died last night."

Rebekah Winslow visibly flinched. "He got to live out his last days in peace. He never paid for his crimes."

"I am sorry for what he has done. I cannot erase his past. I am not here for that reason." Daniel lifted the box for emphasis. Its musty smell permeated the air. The cardboard was beginning to rot, and the edges were fortified with packing tape. "My mother brought this to me today."

"I don't see any relevance."

"There is nothing I can do about my grandfather. But there is something I can do. My father was a military man. These are his papers from 1983, the last year of the Dirty War."

"I don't know what that is," she said, furtively glancing at Eleanor, but her stance remained stiff.

"The military took over Argentina in 1976. Torture became the norm."

"You willingly admit your father was a part of this?"

"I don't know exactly what he did, but he played his part. He believed, like my grandfather, that order is best kept with fear and cruelty. Military force was the best way to rule. My dad is in a home now out in Middleburg. He has early-onset Alzheimer's."

"Another family member who so easily escapes justice. And what about you? What is it you do? Steal babies? Ruin families? Install military bases in select cities?"

Eleanor's mouth dropped open. "Mother." Maybe it was not a good idea to bring Daniel over, but she remembered a proverb from her bubbe, her grandmother: If the goat didn't jump, it would have a miserable life.

Daniel continued doggedly. "There is a curse on my family." He relaxed his stance by sitting on a nearby barstool. "My brother Thomas and my sister Camila died within a year of each other. My mother was grief-stricken. She made my father take a job in the embassy to leave Argentina. She thought that was the answer. But you see it as running. Am I right?"

Mama nodded stiffly.

"Perhaps there is truth in that," he acknowledged. Eleanor could see a slight release of tension in her mother's body. "I have a chance now to help others rectify the past and hopefully remove the curse."

Mama zeroed in on him as if she were a cobra ready to strike. "How can you do that? You carry the sins of your grandfather and your father. You cannot make it right. Your family deserves this curse."

"I was contacted by the Grandmothers of the Plaza. Do you know who they are?" He waited for her response.

A blank look crossed her face.

"During the war, many leftist rebels were killed. Their children were stolen and given to other families. These women of the Plaza, they came together because they realized not all hope is lost. They let the children know the truth of their biological parents. Now more than thirty years have passed. The babies are grown up. Even so, the Grandmothers' goal is to reunite the stolen children with their remaining family."

Mama uncrossed her arms at this and cocked her head. "How can you help them?"

"This box and several others belonged to my father. Documentation from the time of the military junta. My mother brought me this one from 1983, the year of my birth and the last year of the war."

"Are you one of the stolen babies?"

"I am going to deliver this box and hopefully the others to the Grandmothers."

"You didn't answer my question."

"I . . ." Daniel paused for a moment, clearly thinking of what he wanted to say before saying it. "Yes, they want me to take a genetic test."

"Will you?"

"You know my mother has lost all her children except me? She is afraid to lose me too. What do you think I should do?"

"I . . ." Mama stood tall and wiped her hands on the apron. "I would not wish that on any mother, but the truth must be known."

"That is why I am taking the DNA test."

"I see." Mama tilted her head, seemingly to get a better look at Daniel. She glanced over at Eleanor, who stood quietly in the doorway.

While there were certainly no whoops of joy and camaraderie, the conversation was unfolding in a much more civil manner than Eleanor had expected. Her mother was listening, and Eleanor's heart fluttered with hope.

"Don't you risk jail time in delivering this box?" asked Mama. "Are there repercussions for your bravery?"

"Not likely. Argentinians ache for answers. This will give them some. But the government will not prosecute anyone."

"And then that's it? You wipe away the sins of the father with one box? With one genetic test?"

Silence pervaded the room. Eleanor was afraid that moving would somehow shatter the tenuous threads of respect that seemed to be growing between Daniel and her mother.

"I am doing what I can to help the Grandmothers of the Plaza. My hope is that the documentation will help someone to answer questions, but it may be nothing. My parents kept them all these years, and it was very difficult for my mother to give one to me. But my hope is to help in whatever small way I can."

"I see. And what are your intentions with my daughter?"

"She helped me to see what I should do."

"How do you mean?"

Daniel placed both hands on his knees and rubbed his legs as if he were getting ready to perform a difficult physical task. He looked Mama in the eye. "My whole life, people who had been harmed by my grandfather and my father were simply . . . other people. I didn't have personal contact with them that I was aware of and certainly even less so in the United

States. When I met Eleanor and learned about her past, I began to see. She is like a light in a dark room."

Mama smiled for the first time, the corners of her lips barely turning up. "That is what Eleanor's name means. It means shining light, the bright one."

Daniel turned to look at Eleanor. "That is what she is," he said, smiling. Then he turned back. "I love your daughter, Mrs. Winslow. I'd do anything for her."

Heat rose from Eleanor's chest up into her throat. She had strong feelings for him but was afraid to call it love. Now that he had said it, in front of her mother, she was no longer anxious of her feelings.

"I'm not sure if love is the right word." Her mother's expression softened, and her shoulders relaxed. She took a deep breath. "Perhaps it is too soon for this word. But you'd do anything for her. Is that true?"

"Yes, anything," he said, his eyes leaving hers.

"Would you convert to Judaism?"

Eleanor couldn't believe her mother would ask him. He wouldn't want to marry her if he understood what would be required of him.

He replied swiftly and surely. "If we decided to get married someday, that is something I would do."

Rebekah had a twinkle in her eye as if she had caught the fox in the henhouse. Eleanor knew what was coming next. She straightened her back and watched Daniel.

"Converting also means you would need to become circumcised. Would you do that as well?"

"Well . . ." Daniel hesitated. Eleanor could feel her heart thumping wildly in her chest.

"Would you?" Mama asked, her eyebrows furrowing.

"It's a lot to ask of someone, but . . ." Daniel put both hands in front of his face with his thumbs to his lips, almost like he was praying. A look of calm came over him. "Yes, Mrs. Winslow, I would do that for her. It's only a piece of skin."

Rebekah Winslow's mouth dropped, but she recovered quickly. "Well, then," she picked up the electric teapot that Eleanor had started and lifted it. "I'll believe it when I see it. But for now would you like some tea?"

Daniel took a quick peek back at Eleanor and grinned. Would he really get circumcised for her? Or was he saying it to appease her mother? He appeared to be genuine. Words mattered to him. Eleanor took three ceramic cups and a box of tea out of the cupboard.

Mama took off her apron and dusted the remaining flour off. "You seem like a good man, Daniel. I cannot believe how difficult this must be for you and for your mother."

"To do nothing would be more difficult," he replied.

"Daniel," Mama said, taking off her apron and laying it on the counter, "I am a stubborn woman, and I won't change overnight. But let's see what happens."

"Perhaps love might not be so bad," she said, placing her hand on her daughter's cheek. "My own life was terrible, and he seems to be--"

"A good man. I love you, Mama." Eleanor gave her mother a strong hug, holding her tight.

"A lot has happened, and I'm very tired. I'm going to go home. Call me later?" she asked, grasping Eleanor's hand. Eleanor squeezed back with a silent nod.

"Daniel, thank you for coming here and explaining. That could not have been easy," Mama said, patting his shoulder.

"It's fine, Mrs. Winslow. I appreciate your words."

With a nod, Mama excused herself. "Oh, and Eleanor, finish the bialys, please. Be sure to wrap some for Daniel and his mother." She smiled softly and headed to the front door, shutting it softly behind her.

Chapter 28

Eleanor and Daniel stood in the kitchen, a little bit in awe and a little bit in shock. "That went better than expected," said Eleanor, pulling the towel-covered bowl toward her to check the dough. "I didn't think she'd ever come around, let alone that easily."

"We'll get our mothers together for a more formal introduction. My mama will take some time, but she'll come around too."

Eleanor took the towel off the bowl and touched it to see if it had risen enough. "When you said you loved me. Did you mean it?"

"Look at me, Eleanor." When she met his eyes, he stepped backwards. "I knew after our first night together."

"But how can you be sure?"

"If you're asking for a logical answer, I don't have one." He shrugged and rolled his shoulders. "But I trust my heart. Respect, admiration—those take time. But I had a feeling that you were special." He walked to her and kissed her on the forehead. "Would you mind if I take a shower? And I'd like to borrow your robe."

"My pink robe?"

"Yes, it fits me perfectly."

"You may, Daniel Prado." He gave her a hug, a full body hug which made her feel so close to him as if nothing could come between them. She knew everything would be all right. They could take their relationship to the next level without any concerns about hidden truths or expectations--the kind of relationship she wanted.

After a kiss on her cheek, he went upstairs. She picked up the kitchen and finished making the bialys, putting them into the oven. She set a timer that would automatically shut off the oven. She headed upstairs to change into yoga pants and a T-shirt printed with an advertisement for a Polish beer that she liked. She lay down on her bed with a magazine while waiting for the bialys to bake.

"You look beautiful, *galgita*," Daniel said, appearing in the doorway. His hair was wet and slicked back. The robe was lightly tied at his waist. "You like my robe, no?"

"Pink is your color."

She moved so she was at the foot of the bed. He came inside the bedroom, and his hand settled on her waist. "Is this what you want?"

"Yes." She lifted her T-shirt up and he pulled it off, never once releasing her gaze. The olive color of his skin contrasted to the lightness of her own. He slipped his fingers around the waistband of her yoga pants and glided them down. She let them fall and kicked them to the side. She untied his robe and pushed the fabric away from his body but not off.

There was no sound except the rustling of clothes. They stood there in each other's presence, not knowing what to say but understanding everything that was unspoken. She relaxed into him, and they fell onto the bed.

They kissed each other and tongues tasted each other, exploring. He pinched and twisted her nipple with one hand while his stout cock nudged between her swollen labia. She opened her thighs, already wet and ready for him. He slid into her tight pussy, hard and deep. She arched back at the sensuous pleasure, the filling of her, the way he touched her core in a way that only he could.

He pulled out slowly and exquisitely, his eyes

intent on her, and slammed back into her. Obliterated, that was how she felt as he built into a syncopated rhythm, thrusting deeper and deeper. She was inundated by overwhelming sensations of pleasure and lust and love mixed with hope and friendship. She trusted him completely. This was love. This was what she had been missing her whole life.

She ran her fingers lightly over his shoulder blades, watching as he curved his back before coming into her, the force lifting her hands away from him for a moment. She was about to orgasm, the edge of it riding up her legs like a rising tide. His movements quickened until she burst into a million pieces. Somehow, he was smashing her apart and putting her back together in the same moment, changing destiny to a future they could have.

She called out his name. His muscled body rose into the air, and she could feel the power in his thighs, in his haunches, and then he was coming too in one final explosion. After the waves subsided, they both caught their breath.

"Darling *galgita*, my lover," he said, smiling at her and whisking a stray hair out of her eyes, "my light."

Eleanor reached around him and held him close. There was nothing between them, and yet he was everything.

More by Juno Chase

The DC Knights series can be read in any order, but we hope you don't miss any of them!

New to the Game—D.C. Knights Book 1

Chloe's the new intern, but she jumps into the game both feet first.

Playing For Keeps—D.C. Knights Book 2

Katherine thinks she's got things figured out until a sexy scientist tangos his way into her heart.

All In—D.C. Knights Book 3

Madeline has no problem playing games until she meets Ewan a man who knows how to treat her like a woman.

Fair and Square—D.C. Knights Book 4

Lizbeth doesn't have time for games, but she ends up in the midst of a political game no one in Congressman Pierce's office saw coming.

Only Bluffing—D.C. Knights Book 5

Eleanor Winslow and Daniel Prado are from different worlds. Will their love overcome dark histories and ancient legacies?

Game On—D.C. Knights Book 6

Cheyenne LeFleur lives on the wild side. Will Alexander Moore be able to handle her history, or will he reject her like so many before him?

For the Win—D.C. Knights Book 7 The final chapter in this series. Congressman Lincoln Pierce deserves love, too. Can he find it while maintaining his principles?

Also by Juno Chase:

ARTIFACT of BETRAYAL: an exciting romantic suspense novel

If you had to choose between saving your life or the love of your life, *who would you choose?*

Claire Townsend has it all, a great job, her own shop in Brooklyn, until one night when she loses everything. With thirteen days to pay off a dangerous loan shark, she decides to partake in a black-market smuggling operation to save her own neck.

Bruno Canul is an archeologist who works as a consultant with the FBI. He chases a suspect to Belize only to find the ex-love-of-his-life as part of the crew. He can't tell if he should trust Claire or if she's joined forces with the smuggler.

Afraid her choices will get Bruno killed, Claire tries to resist falling back in love with him. If she goes through with the smuggling scheme, she can pay off her loan, but she'd lose Bruno's love and trust *forever*. If she stands up for their love, she's a dead woman.

This adventurous romantic suspense is sure to keep you on the edge of your seat as Claire and Bruno find love in the jungle and ancient Mayan ruins of Belize.

About Juno Chase

Who said chivalry is dead? They were totally wrong! We love, love, love hot guys who are modern day knights and heroes but also know how to heat things up between the sheets.

Juno Chase is the nom de plume of two married moms who love reading and writing happy stories. We wanted to see these modern day knights celebrated in romance, so here we are. We're not a big group of people writing—there is just the two of us. We both spend lots of time reading and writing in each story to bring you the most complete, hot, and exciting stories possible.

Thank you so much for reading *New to the Game*, we hope you enjoyed reading it as much as we did writing it. If you sign up for our newsletter, you will be the first to know whenever we have a new book available.

Follow Juno Chase on your favorite social Media. We'd love to hear from you!

www.Junochase.com

juno@junochase.com

Acknowledgments

We'd like to thank a few people who helped us get this book into your lovely hands, dear readers. We are part of an amazing writing group who has listened to our ideas, helped us with plotting, and given us some straight feedback. We couldn't have done this without your energy and help-—you ladies rock! Thank you for all your reading time and thoughtful suggestions to help make the D.C. Knights series a reality.

To our intrepid beta readers. Thank you for taking the time to read and give us honest criticism. Especially to Dawn who has faithfully read everything we've handed her and keeps asking for more!

And to our families—our fabulous husbands and children who have supported us in so many different ways and picked up the pieces as needed. We love you!